ABOUT THIS BOOK

From *USA Today* bestselling author Morgan Wylie comes a new story in the saga of the Havenwood Falls Blackstone witch hunters.

Brice Blackstone is a black sheep, born with dark hair and the only male ever marked as a witch hunter in Havenwood Falls. He now knows there are others, but as his powers are reawakening, he fears what will happen. After all, the other males are rogues, assassins not only after witches but all supernatural kind. And nobody knows what to expect with him since—as he's heard throughout his whole life—he is different.

His experiences are definitely different. Strange dreams. Voices in his head. The help he secretly accepts from an unlikely source. And then there's the way he reacts to the surprise visitor, opposite of everyone else.

Sunny is an anomaly. Always has been. Dante, leader of the rogue hunters, let her march to her own drum, as she's a valued member of his crew. So when she shows up in Havenwood Falls, Brice's family goes on full alert.

Brice believes in Sunny, though. She knows things nobody else does—like how he can control the witch hunter within before it takes control of him. And in a town full of witches, he must master himself or lose everything he knows and loves.

REDISCOVERED

MORGAN WYLIE

HAVENWOOD FALLS HIGH BOOKS

Paper Bird by Amy Richie

Predestined by Valia Lind

Rediscovered by Morgan Wylie

Stay up to date at www.HavenwoodFalls.com

Subscribe to our reader group and receive free stories and more!

BOOKS BY MORGAN WYLIE

YA FANTASY:

Silent Orchids (Book 1)

Veiled Shadows (Book 2)

Daegan (Novella 2.5)

Fractured Darkness (Book 3)

Fading Light (Book 4)

The Sol-Lumieth (Forthcoming)

The Rise of the Paladin (An Alandria Short Story Prequel ~ Free with Newsletter subscription)

YA PARANORMAL/SUPERNATURAL:: HAILEY: THE NECROMANCER (A SHADOW REALM NOVELLA 1)

JAX: The Doppelgänger (A Shadow Realm Novella 2)

WILLOW (A Shadow Realm Novella 3) (Forthcoming)

SOLANGE: (A Shadow Realm Novella 4) (Forthcoming)

NA/ADULT PARANORMAL ROMANCE:: RYLEN (THE TANGLED WEB BOOK 1)

MATHER (The Tangled Web Book 2)

JET (A Tangled Web Novella)

ENOCK (Forthcoming)

LUCIUS (Forthcoming)

To all the loyal HF readers, I hope you enjoy this next story in the saga of the Havenwood Falls Blackstone witch hunters.

CHAPTER 1

"Come on, Brice, don't be a baby!" a guy from school taunted from the other side of the fence enclosing the skate park located in Danzan Park. Chadwick Linton was a basketball jock, a witch, and a jerk. Brice ignored him, but a tingling sensation he had never felt before started in the palms of his hands, then moved into his wrists and up his forearms. Brice instinctively flexed his hands and swallowed a gasp. The sensation in his forearms was the telltale sign a witch hunter felt when in a witch's presence.

Could he be transitioning right here, right now? He was almost eighteen, after all, and that was the golden age when the witch hunters from his family tended to come into their own. He knew some of what might happen from his sister Macy's experience when the witch hunter reawakened within her, but he was different. Or so he'd been told all his life. Brice didn't know *all* of what to expect, so he couldn't be sure his transition had begun. He shook his hands out, trying to make the tingles go away, but Chadwick was too close to him.

Head in the game. The only way out of there was to skate his way out. Otherwise, he wouldn't outlive the jokes and comments from the other guys. The skateboard world could be tough, even in Havenwood Falls. Either you were a skateboarder or you were a poser. Brice wasn't a poser.

"You've done harder tricks than that. Don't get psyched out!" another guy shouted from the sidelines. Brice recognized all the kids there. Most were classmates he'd known the majority of his life, either from attending Havenwood Falls High School or more recently from the private school, Sun and Moon Academy. Out of the corner of his eye, he noted Jordan Woods hanging out in his football jersey, surrounded by Zoey Mills, Emma Cardin, and Celeste Long, along with the newer guy, Jonathan Burns.

Brice had gone to Havenwood Falls High—the public school—since he was a freshman, but the family, concerned for what might happen when he did transition, pulled Brice out of Havenwood Falls High his senior year and enrolled him in the private school. They gave explicit instructions to the headmaster to not put Brice in any classes with witches. As the witch-to-anything-else ratio at the Academy was higher than at the public school, Brice ended up with a lot of independent study time for his senior year.

His older brother, Brock, who now runs Soothing Sips tasting room in the town square, also attended the public school, so Brice was bummed to be the only one in his family who wouldn't be a Havenwood Falls High graduate. He hated leaving some of his friends, but the truth was he liked the change of pace at the Academy. He had more freedom and independence. Some thought the private school was for troubled kids who couldn't control their magic—and maybe that was the case—but others attended whose parents wanted to keep their kids more exclusive to the supernatural sector.

Brice's friend Samuel Milton, who didn't ride a skateboard, stood behind him with a few others, including Cade Peters, a hellhound a couple years younger from his new school. Dalton Underwood, a Havenwood Falls High sophomore, stood nearby with his board, waiting his turn. They had set up a bit of a practice competition and invited a bunch of people to come out and watch. For the middle of October, it was an unusually pleasant afternoon, and all the kids wanted to be outside after school.

Samuel playfully punched the back of Brice's bicep.

"Don't listen to 'em, Brice. Don't do it if you don't feel it," he encouraged with whispered vigor. Samuel Milton still attended HFH, and Brice had missed hanging out with him every day. Samuel was a lynx shifter and also Macy's best friend Ruby Jean's little brother, so they had practically grown up together. But Samuel didn't understand the skateboarding culture, nor the pressure to perform in a way to prove legitimacy.

Brice cringed inside, knowing the other guys would make fun of him if they heard Samuel attempting to help him back out. The last thing Brice wanted was to back out. He knew he could make the run; it was a standard drop into the bowl, maneuver some tricks, then make his way through the half pipe and finally complete the course with tricks on the rails. But something inside him held him back.

And that made him mad.

Brice wasn't a chicken. He was a good skateboarder, one of the best in Havenwood Falls, in fact. Quickly he glanced all around him to ensure nothing littered the ramps. While doing so, he noticed the Blaekthorn twins—wolf shifters, Weston and Drake—standing nearby, as well as other kids, including Gianna Augustine and Aurelia Petran. Another girl named Ellie Lewis stood by, which made him smile. She'd had a rough past couple years losing her brother, and he hadn't seen her much.

Halloween was quickly approaching, and in Havenwood Falls, even the playground got decorated. He chuckled internally, then got back to business. If he didn't make the drop soon, his spot would be taken by another rider, and he'd be out of the competition, forever seen as a coward.

"I'm going!" he announced, swiping the floppy dark hair from his forehead and taking a deep breath. *Piece of cake.*

Brice jumped on his custom-designed skateboard, dropped into the bowl just deep and wide enough to gain momentum before attempting to stall at the top edge rail, then back down into the depths of the bowl for another round. Once out of the bowl, he did a kick turn and flew down the ramp, dropping into the lower half-pipe, gaining speed as he went. From there he'd complete the course with kick turns and tricks from grinding the axle of his board on the rails to grabbing his board in the air for a 180 turn. He had visualized this moment over and over again. It was a no-brainer in his mind.

His mom would freak if she knew he didn't wear his helmet, but he never did and neither did the other "real" skateboarders. It was one less thing they could make fun of him for. It wasn't like he really cared what they thought, but he didn't want to be *that* guy—the one who always obeyed the rules, the one who always listened to his mommy, the one who still answered to his parents. He wasn't a rebel by a long shot, but he still had moments where he felt like he wanted to be one.

His mom rode his ass like no one else in his family. She was overbearing and treated him like a baby. Lilith Blackstone might sit on the Court of the Sun and the Moon, but she didn't need to dictate his life. After all, he was going to be eighteen soon, and then he could move out and live his own life just like Macy had wanted to, except this time he was prepared for his hunter awakening—at least as much as he could be, being the only male witch hunter in Havenwood Falls.

After Macy had left Havenwood Falls a few years ago, afraid of what her hunter side would become, she made sure her family told Brice everything he needed to know. Brice appreciated that she cared so much, but he didn't understand what the big deal was anyhow or why they made it an event to awaken the hunter. From Macy's stories, he knew the rogue Blackstone witch hunters had other males, and their gifts weren't suppressed early on. They grew up knowing all about themselves and their talents and what they could do. Brice didn't want to be a witch hunter in the sense the rogues were, but he didn't understand why his family made it such a big deal in Havenwood Falls.

Brice made several smaller jumps and did some tricks along the way as he gained speed and confidence leading up to the big jumps at the end. He heard a group cheering off to the side. He turned his head and gave the ladies on the sideline a tip of his head. He should focus but wanted to be the cocky jock type just for a moment. But when he looked, he caught only one set of eyes in the crowd. Bright blue ones surrounded by light golden-blond hair.

He knew those eyes—witch hunter eyes—though he didn't know

who they belonged to. His vision tunneled as his eyes locked onto hers. Electrical shocks sizzled across the back of his neck. Definitely a hunter, one he didn't know.

Brice flew through the air. The ground went out from underneath him. The girl made him feel weightless like he could fly. Or perhaps he was flying.

Her blue eyes went wide, and her face paled more than it already was.

"BRICE!" several voices screamed from somewhere in the distance. Brice couldn't understand what was happening. He felt like everything moved in slow motion. Life had suddenly become crystal clear. He wanted to be free to be all he could be. All the bottled up potential he felt brewing inside him was ready. This was his time. His body tickled with energy surging through from his head down to his toes. Tingles shot up and down his arms. Witches were near. He had never fully felt them before. Maybe he would finally discover the kind of hunter he would become. Maybe this was his awakening.

Instant pain replaced euphoric energy.

"Dude! You flew!" said a voice Brice recognized but couldn't put a name to.

"Are you messed up, bro?" a rather hesitant male voice asked. "What were you doing?"

"Brice, can you hear me?" an unfamiliar female voice called as if she pushed her way through to him with those bright blue eyes.

"Brice, are you all right?" a separate male voice said, filled with panic.

"Keep him still. I called the clinic." That had to be Ellie Lewis. Her stepfather was a doctor at the clinic.

"And I called his mom," a voice—Samuel—offered. Of course Samuel called his mom. He was going to be in so much shit, but until the pain subsided, he wasn't sure he really cared.

Then darkness replaced the pain, and he felt no more.

CHAPTER 2

*B*rice heard heavy breathing and the occasional snore. Keeping his eyes closed, he took a moment to listen for the beeping sound of machines. Not hearing anything, he figured he wasn't at the medical clinic. Peeking between his lids, he spied his older brother Brock sprawled out in the corner chair, dead asleep. Brice breathed deeply and filled his chest with relief until the truth of his situation dawned on him—he was in his own room at his house, meaning his mom knew what had happened.

What had happened? Brice tried to remember what went down at the skate park. All he could remember were bright blue eyes hypnotizing him—that must have caused him to fall!

He tried to sit up, but quickly lay back down. His head swam and pain shot up his arm. He couldn't help the groan that escaped his throat.

"Hey, slugger," his brother said, his eyes shooting open. He stretched like a feline. "You broke your wrist."

"I can feel that," Brice said dryly, his head lolling in his brother's direction.

"The doc gave you some pain meds, and Mom has a salve from the Luna Coven that will help your wrist heal quickly, but she wants to talk to you before she gives it to you."

Brice groaned with a different kind of pain, and his head fell back against his pillow.

"You messed up, little brother. I know you don't wear a helmet when you're with the guys, but Mom's gonna kill you for it. You're lucky you didn't do more damage. In fact, we aren't sure how you got out with only a broken wrist, unless perhaps there was some magical assistance in cushioning your fall."

"I felt magic. And I felt the presence of a witch."

"Like more than usual? Your hunter gifts starting to reawaken?" His brother sat forward, concerned anticipation etched on his face.

"Maybe? I'm not sure. That thought ran through my head when I fell, but now I'm not sure."

"What do you remember?" Brock prodded.

"Blue eyes," Brice let slip, and the blush invading his face revealed it to his brother, too.

"Blue eyes, huh? Well, that's an interesting detail to remember. They belong to anyone in particular?"

Brice slowly shook his head. "I don't know. I just saw her on the sidelines while I was riding."

"Ah. So she was the distraction. I knew you were better than to fall on that jump." Brock shook his head in denial but then let out a laugh. "I can't believe my little brother got sidelined by blue eyes. I never thought I'd see the day. I thought for sure you'd end up single, sitting in the basement playing video games the rest of your miserable life."

"Shut up, Brock. Why are you here anyway?" Brice threw a pillow at his brother. The truth was, he much preferred having his brother than his mom sitting there when he woke up. At least this way, he could gauge her response before he had to take her on.

"Mom had to run to the vineyard to help cover NamaStays Inn for Grandma while she had a meeting regarding the new school year." Brock huffed. "I still can't believe Grandma is going to try teaching at the new Sun & Moon Academy College. I can't wait to hear from Macy and Gallad how she does at it."

"I know, right?" Brice laughed, then winced, wishing he hadn't, as he gripped his left wrist to keep from moving it wrong. Brice found the image of her teaching weapons to be comical—not that she couldn't do it justice but because she looked like a pretentious woman of wealth who wouldn't be caught dead holding anything as barbaric as a sword, especially one worn and bloodied from battle. "I can't wait to see that myself."

"You'll be lucky if Mom lets you live long enough to even graduate," Brock goaded.

"You gonna let her kill me, Brock?"

"He might not have a choice in the matter," his mom's voice came from the open doorway, down the hall.

Brice closed his eyes and groaned again.

"Didn't know you were coming back so soon, Mom," Brock sheepishly acknowledged as his eyes widened like a kid caught in the act.

"Macy came to take over at the inn, so I came back to see if Brice had woken up." Lilith came fully into the doorway. Her eyes quickly took in her son lying on the bed, and though her face held little concern or emotion at all, the fear behind her eyes subsided once she saw him. Lilith Blackstone was a tall, thin, authoritative woman. She loved her family fiercely, but everything about her screamed fierce. To Brice's knowledge, there had never been a soft edge on his mom. She loved them and took care of them, but if it weren't for the softer, caring side of his father, Reggie, they might have been more messed up as children. As it was, they had their issues, but overall he thought his family was pretty cool.

"Are you in pain, Brice?" she asked with some concern.

"Some. But I can feel the meds helping too," he quietly answered her.

"Good." She was back to business. "What the hell were you thinking out there?" She didn't yell, but sometimes he wished she would. It always felt like the perfect storm brewing with her, ready to burst open at any moment and drown them all in it.

"That I could do it."

"Without your helmet?"

Brice looked away, knowing he was wrong, but still had to try like the high school boy he was. "The other guys don't wear theirs—you're not considered a *real* skater if you wear one, and I knew I could do it."

"But you didn't."

"I would have been able to, if I hadn't been distracted," Brice said with a frustrated huff.

"By a pair of pretty blue eyes, no less," Brock offered as only a big brother could—with a dramatic teasing flare.

"Whose blue eyes?" Lilith asked, not missing a beat.

Brice locked his face down with a tight frown, glaring at Brock. Then he shifted his gaze to his mom's and sighed, knowing she wouldn't let him off that easy.

"I don't know. I haven't seen her before, but she had hunter eyes, and I could feel her presence. I haven't been able to do that yet, but I did. Does that mean my hunter gene is kicking in?" Brice hoped offering a different subject would get him off the hook about the girl, but no such luck.

"A witch hunter girl? Here in Havenwood Falls? One you don't know?" Lilith interrogated, suddenly on high alert.

Brice shrugged. "Yes, I didn't know her. She was off to the side of the skate area. I didn't talk to her or anything."

"But you felt her?"

Brice nodded.

"Well, perhaps it is your time, Brice. Keep me informed as you experience different changes in your body so we can gauge if your transformation is any different than any of ours." Lilith stood to leave. She expected full participation.

"This is almost worse than puberty." Brice fell back against his pillow. "You're going to hound me, aren't you?"

Every witch hunter in Havenwood Falls was born with a natural mark indicating they would have hunter abilities. However, at a young age, they were given a second temporary mark to subdue the hunter tendencies. Being surrounded by witches was hard enough as an adult witch hunter in control, but a young one having to encounter witches daily would have a hard time controlling their urges. So for the greater good of the community and for the young hunter, they were marked with a ward to prevent possible issues. Around their eighteenth year, the hunter began to emerge as the ward wore off. They learned to control the strong sensations and urges to attack every witch they encountered. Then the hunter had the choice to stay and receive their permanent marking as a resident of the town, also taking the edge off their urges, or they could choose to leave.

"It's not hounding, son. It's making sure you enter into your powers as a witch hunter with all the grace I know you are capable of, even without a crash helmet on." She gave him a sarcastic smile, ruffled his hair, then turned to leave the room.

He knew she wasn't going to let go of him not wearing his helmet. At least she didn't make a bigger deal about the girl. He still wondered who she was and if he'd get to see her again. Something about her drew him in, and he wanted to know what she was doing in Havenwood Falls.

CHAPTER 3

*B*rice woke up drenched from a cold sweat to find himself still in his room, but the view outside the window revealed night had finally come. He hadn't meant to fall asleep, but the meds he'd been given made him deliriously sleepy . . . so much so, his dream could be explained away. Brice steadied his heartbeat.

"It was just a dream, a crazy messed up dream, but only a dream," he said to himself as he shook the rest of his sleep away. Stiff and sore, Brice slowly stretched what limbs he could and made his way off his bed and into the attached bathroom. His stomach growled, and he was grateful to feel a little more himself.

On his way downstairs to the kitchen to find the rest of the family and some food, he realized that his mom forgot to give him the healing salve for his wrist. He was just about to yell out to see where his family members were when he heard hushed voices coming from the downstairs den: his mom, Macy, and another female voice growing in familiarity—Hollis Blackstone.

Hollis had only come to Havenwood Falls in the last six months from the rogue witch hunter group headed by Dante Blackstone, her father. She was sent in as a spy but defected and chose to change her ways as a hunter, fell in love with Ryne Calloway—a half witch, half phoenix—and chose to remain in Havenwood Falls with no further attachments to her dad or the *other* Blackstones. He knew many still were skeptical about her, but he liked her. She brought a fresh perspective to their home and added another level of attitude to stand up to his mom when called for.

"Brice saw her at the skate park," Lilith stated.

Brice wondered who and why they were talking about him and some girl at all. Did they mean the girl he saw with the bright blue eyes? The girl who caused his wreck?

"Who?" Macy innocently asked. He would thank Macy when he saw her.

"She's here?" Hollis returned.

"Who's here?" Macy again, with a little more frustration.

"Did you know she was coming?" His mom.

Brice wondered about the girl even more now. Where was she from? Since Hollis was brought in on the discussion, he was curious if the girl was from the rogue Blackstones. But Dante's group had no way of knowing where Havenwood Falls was located or how to find it, unless someone told them, but no one there would tell anyone—under penalty of possible death. The supernatural residents of Havenwood Falls took their secrecy and privacy extremely seriously.

"No. I had no idea. Does the Court think I did?" Hollis asked with added panic. Brice knew if she broke her agreement with the Court, she would be kicked out of Havenwood Falls for good with no memory of ever being there.

"Not yet, but they will wonder how she found us," Lilith concluded.

"I mean, I know I've been busy becoming a guardian at the college and all, but will someone tell me what's going on?" Macy said with exasperation.

"Sunny is in town," Hollis finally answered.

"Sunny? Seriously?" Macy's voice rose with surprise. "I liked Sunny. She helped me when I was with them."

Brice couldn't take it any longer. He entered the room without the girls noticing. "Who is Sunny and why are you making such a fuss about her?"

His mom's lips were pursed in frustration, probably because he had heard them.

"She is one of the rogue witch hunters who used to live with Dante," his mom said matter-of-factly, as if that should explain it all. Since Hollis had encountered her father back in May, Brice had heard rumors of Dante's disappearance: that he had not returned to the other Blackstones. If anyone in Havenwood Falls knew the truth, they weren't sharing it with him.

"How did she find us?" he asked.

"We don't know. She shouldn't have been able to," Hollis said, throwing her long dark hair back over her right shoulder. Brice looked at her eyes. They were the same blue eyes he saw in Sunny, his mom, his sister, his grandma, and any who bore the mark of the witch hunter. He saw those same eyes in the mirror every day.

"Well, has anyone just asked her?" Brice said with a tone that held a hint of the obvious.

The room went silent.

"I haven't seen her, or I'd have asked her," Macy said with a shrug, causing her blond hair tied high on her head to bounce.

"Actually, no one has seen her except you, son," Lilith said with a strange tone, "and also one of the boys who told me about the 'strange girl who approached you after you fell to see if you were all right.'" He hated when his mom used air quotes.

Brice looked at her and cocked his head. "You got Sunny from that information?"

Lilith shifted her feet, slightly uncomfortable. "No. I received a warning from Mathilde Augustine last week. She said we would have a visitor, and she described her to me. You know how Mathilde sometimes has moments of premonition. Well, I didn't think much of it, as I didn't think it was possible for her to find us." She paused and gazed out the window. "But then you mentioned seeing someone who fit her description, and I put them together."

"Detective Mom," Macy said with a giggle, then glanced at Brice with a wink. Lilith responded with an expression akin to an eye roll, without actually stooping to that level.

13

"Anyway, we'd been on the lookout for her but somehow she still got in unnoticed until recently, and for some reason she sought you out first . . . I wonder why?" Lilith took on an inquisitive look with her hands placed upon her hips.

"Maybe she didn't seek me out, but stumbled upon the skate park and happened to arrive in time to see me," Brice offered, but his words lacked conviction.

Hollis shrugged but shook her head. "No, Sunny is anything but random. She can be quirky and strange and seem haphazard, but everything she does is with purpose. I have lived with Sunny her entire life, and I still don't understand her. There is something unique about her. For example, Dante never treated her the same as everyone else. She's always been special. I thought at one point, there might be something mentally unpredictable about her, but it seems she just moves to the beat of her own drum . . . and Dante always let her."

"Interesting," Lilith mumbled under her breath.

"When I was there, she was so sweet to me and made a point to help me understand that I did not, in fact, kill a witch they tried to convince me I had killed in order to break me. She didn't have to do that," Macy added.

"I'll let the Court know," Lilith said. She pulled her phone out from her jacket pocket, texted something short, then put her phone back.

Brice grew more intrigued the more they spoke of Sunny. He couldn't wait to meet her and see what kind of drama a cute, petite teenage girl could stir up.

"Hey, Mom, I was looking for you to see if I could get the healing salve for my arm so it heals faster," Brice changed the subject, pointing at his injured and wrapped wrist.

Lilith slowly moved her vision to hold only Brice—the effect was unnerving as only a mom could do. He had a bad feeling.

"Your father and I talked about it. Since you heal relatively quick, we decided to let the natural consequences of what you did sink in, so you will make a smarter decision next time regarding your helmet."

"What? You're not going to give it to me? I just have to let it heal like a human . . . all slow and natural?" Brice guffawed.

Macy giggled under her breath but apparently couldn't help but let it slip out a bit. Brice glared at her.

"You know what I mean. Why wouldn't we use the healing gift when it's been offered?" he whined.

"You have medication from the doctor for your pain. It will not hurt you more than you can handle to wait a few days."

Brice dropped his head to his chest in utter despair and defeat as only a teenager could.

"You can get through this, little brother!" Macy annoyingly cheerfully patted him on his good shoulder, then headed out the door toward the kitchen. "Come on, I'll make you some food."

"Macy, why aren't you at college anyway?" Brice asked suddenly, realizing she probably shouldn't be home. Macy moved into the dorm when she got accepted into SMA for the year and hadn't been around much with her full schedule.

"That school is insane. A lot of dark energy with some weird stuff happening. I just needed a break, get out of the mountain, you know. Plus I had to come check on my little brother to make sure he wasn't brain damaged, but I think it was already too late for that," she said and laughed from down the hall.

After Macy left, Brice turned back to his mom. He wanted to say something to his mother, but when he looked at her, he knew there was no argument, and he sighed with resignation. He wished his dad had been there. He might have been able to persuade his dad to see his side: the side who'd have to go to school and face the others with his screw up . . . again. He just wanted to fit in, and somehow he figured this would do the exact opposite of that. So instead, he went to drown out his frustrations with whatever food his sister would make him.

CHAPTER 4

The next day, his mom kept Brice home from school to ensure he was fully recovered—except for his wrist, which was going to take much longer since he wasn't allowed to use the magical ointment. He grumbled all morning and knew he was surly to his parents, probably contributing to their speedy exit to Stone Falls Winery to check on "things," but he was miserable, and he wanted them to know it. In the end, the only person it was truly annoying was himself, since everyone had left.

Looking out the window, he saw dark clouds rolling in. Up that high in the mountains, the snows usually came early, and he was ready to hit the half pipe up on the mountain. Snowboarding wasn't much different from skateboarding, and he loved them both. It was a sport he actually felt competent at. The skate park was still open this time of year due to "in-ground heating," also known as a little magic from the covens to keep the ground from freezing. Skating had been a lifeline for him. Life for him in Havenwood Falls was everything he loved. His brother Brock had gone away to college for a short term but ended up coming back because he, too, loved the town. Macy had always wanted to leave, but when she did, it was to escape her fear of becoming a witch hunter because their mom hadn't prepared her for what was to come. But Brice loved everything about where they lived and all he

could experience. He only wished he understood more about himself and who he was meant to be.

Brice was the *great mystery* among their family. With dark hair, he defied all the Blackstones who had hailed from Havenwood Falls. And until Macy had visited the rogue hunters a couple years ago, they thought Brice was some kind of anomaly, being the first male they knew marked as a hunter, and on top of that, one with dark hair. He didn't think it was a big deal, but everything seemed to be a big deal in his family. Brice didn't even care if he became a witch hunter. His brother Brock and his dad weren't. He was content to just play video games, skateboard, and have a good time. The revelation that he had to grow up swiftly approached as he was now a senior in high school, but he had been putting it off as long as he could. Plus, he figured, the plan for his life was all laid out for him by his mom anyway: graduate from high school, then go to work on the family vineyard. Now, with the Sun & Moon Academy College of Supernatural Guardians open for young adults after high school, he had another option to at least prolong starting work at the vineyard. Not that he didn't want to join the family business. He thought their businesses rocked. And since Brock had been experimenting with microbrews, he hoped to join his brother in that endeavor and maybe even open their own side business. Of course, he hadn't talked to Brock or his parents about his venture idea, but in his mind *The Blackstone Brothers Brewery* had a nice ring to it.

But more than anything, he wanted to not be the odd man out. He didn't feel any real sense of purpose or drive to anything special. Even throughout high school, he had been labeled "the loner" or "the skate dork" by those other than his friends. He had dated some, but none of the girls at school really caught his eye.

Until those blue eyes at the skate park.

Brice relocated from the interior great room of his house and stepped outside onto their large covered deck with an amazing view of the town square. The town was decked out with decorations for fall, but especially for the upcoming celebration for Halloween. Havenwood Falls loved Halloween and went all out for it. All the lampposts were tied up with bows in oranges and purples to match the bunting draped across the buildings and signs for each business around the square. It really was a magical time of year for their town, especially the supernaturals. From his vantage point, he could also see people going about their day, and he wondered, if Sunny was in town, what she was doing.

With nothing else to do for the day—unable to play video games or do much of anything with his broken wrist—he settled himself on the comfortable exterior couch, took his pain meds, and laid his head back for a nap.

~

"Brice," a voice whispered through the dark cavern of his mind. Though it was hard to decipher the gender of the voice, it grew in strength and clarity. *"Brice, I know what you want. I know what you need to be free, to be truly all you were meant to be."*

Brice, lost in a sea of darkness and confusion in his mind, called out into the void. "Who are you? Where are you?"

"It doesn't matter who I am, but know that I'm close, closer than you think. And I have the answers you've been seeking, the answers to why . . ." The voice trailed off as if the connection had been severed.

Brice sat up in a rush, frantically looking around him, only to find he was still on the couch outside on the deck of his own house. He had fallen asleep.

He groaned and flopped back onto the cushion, wiping the sweat off his head with his free arm. "Only a dream. What is in those pain meds?"

Brice gathered himself, then got up to get a glass of water from the kitchen, only to find the front door inside his house opening.

His mom, Aunt Letti, and Hollis walked in like a gaggle of geese one after the other. Internally, he rolled his eyes. He did not want to have to converse with them at the moment. He loved them all, but before his dream, he'd been enjoying the solitude of his home. After Hollis walked in, however, another shock of blond hair came around the corner into the great room from the hall. She observed the home with such focused attention, she didn't even see him until their eyes met.

Bright blue eyes. Her eyes. Sunny.

And she was definitely that. Everything about her appearance and disposition was bright and electric. Somehow even her mid-length blond hair appeared shinier than the others.

Brice inhaled sharply; an electric shock ran through his body. *What the F was that?* he wondered internally. He'd never had anything like that happen before.

Oblivious to what he had felt, his mom began introductions.

"Brice, this is Sunny. Sunny, this is my youngest, Brice."

Sunny smiled and rocked onto her toes. "Hello again, Brice. You could have been hurt the other day, but I'm glad you weren't, or things would be much different."

Brice cocked his head, confused, and when he tried to say something in return, he couldn't find the words. He tried to raise his hand in a wave, but he raised the wrong one and pain shot through his arm, and he cried out.

CHAPTER 5

*A*unt Letti clucked her tongue as she moved toward him and held out her hand for the arm he now clutched. "Lilith, why aren't you giving the boy the witch's salve? It would speed up this process so much faster for him."

Brice breathed a sigh of relief. Finally someone was on his side. "Thank you, Aunt Letti, but she won't give it to me."

Lilith scowled at the two of them. "He is being reminded why he should wear a helmet when skating—that could have been your head fractured like that, Brice! Your grandmother is on her way over. Wait until she adds her two cents in."

Brice groaned. He loved his grandma, Eva, but she could be a real tough woman. She had expectations and thought everyone should fall into line accordingly. Brice had heard his mom and dad talking once, and she had explained that Grandma and Aunt Letti were cousins. Eva had wanted to be the family matriarch and sit on the Court, but Letitia was older and got the seat instead. They loved each other, as they'd had over a hundred years to do so, but they had their moments of discord due to very different personality types and ideals.

Brice cleared his throat as he moved to finally get that glass of water he desperately needed. "What brings you all home at this hour of the day?"

"We found Sunny aimlessly wandering around town," Aunt Letti started in.

"Oh, I wasn't aimless, Letti. I was waiting for you to find me," Sunny interjected with a smile, gazing around the room in an almost wistful manner.

"As I said, Sunny never does anything without a reason," Hollis added. "She's very purposeful."

Sunny gave her a deep nod of approval and turned back to the mantel and the family photos she now studied.

"Of course, dear. Well, we found Sunny and decided to bring her back here to have a bit of a chat and get to know her more," Aunt Letti finished.

Brice knew she meant they needed to know why Sunny was in town before they informed the Court of her arrival, so they could determine what should be done. If she was to stay for a bit, they needed to register her as a guest so they could keep tabs on her.

"Sunny?" Hollis walked over to her. Brice knew from Hollis that Sunny had been one of the few she truly cared about. "Sunny, I'm glad to see you, but why are you here? Last time I saw you, you didn't want to come to Havenwood Falls with Ryne and me last summer. Did someone send you?"

"Nope. I told you it wasn't my time before, but now it is. So here I am," she said innocently enough, as if it should be that simple.

Brice leaned over to Aunt Letti, and with his eyes asked the question, *Is she okay?*

Aunt Letti gave him a sharp nod of affirmation.

"How did you get here, dear?" Aunt Letti jumped in before Lilith had the chance.

"Oh!" Sunny smiled and faced them all, her eyes beaming with innocent excitement. "I found a bus with a sign on it. I asked the driver if it would bring me here to you, and he said yes, so I got on."

Lilith cocked her head and stared at Sunny with her eyebrows pinched. "Yes, but how did you find the bus?"

Sunny frowned. "I knew I was supposed to, so I did. Was that wrong?"

Hollis reached over and looped her arm through Sunny's, which made her smile again. "You're fine. Just most people can't find this place. Remember Dante was trying to find it for so long, but couldn't? So they're just curious how you were able to."

"He did have a hard time finding it, didn't he, Holly? I had a map in my head, but I wasn't supposed to tell him, so I didn't. But that's how I found the bus. I followed the map." She tapped her head.

"Good girl, Sunny." Hollis looked to Lilith and then Aunt Letti and shrugged as if asking *what else can you say to that?* It sounded pretty simple. Brice was curious what went on in Sunny's head. She was obviously special, but not in a mentally challenged sort of way. More in a someone-was-telling-her-things-inside-her-head kind of way. He was suddenly struck with a reminder of the dream he had earlier, when someone was talking in his head. So he didn't have much room to speak. Plus, with all the supernaturals they knew, hearing voices or having dreams of premonition were hardly rare—perhaps still uncommon, but the impossible seemed possible in Havenwood Falls. He'd mention that to his mom when Sunny wasn't around.

"Where will you stay while you're here, Sunny?" Brice asked her, once his voice had found its way back.

She smiled at him, and his heart melted. "Holly said I could stay with her!"

Brice looked at Hollis with a sly grin. "Holly, huh?"

"Only to her." She glared at him as if to say, *Don't even try it.* She then turned back to Sunny. "Where are the others? Grace, Nala . . . everybody."

Sunny frowned. "They all argued a lot after Dante didn't come home. Nala thinks she's in charge, but some of the families have disbanded and gone their own way. It's how it's supposed to be for now. It gives them time to try to focus on other matters now instead of hunting witches."

"Where is Dante, if he didn't come home?" Brice genuinely asked. After Hollis was granted permission to stay and got settled, there hadn't been any discussion of Dante or plans to defend the town against him and his rogues. He had forgotten until now to ask about

him. But apparently now was the wrong time to ask, as the room went dead silent. His mom and Aunt Letti exchanged a brief glance, and Hollis chewed her bottom lip, which was very unlike her and very telling at the same time. *Oops.* They probably didn't want to let Sunny and thus the other rogues know if they did something to him.

"We don't exactly know what happened to him," Sunny jumped in, saving them all from having to answer the question. "Some think he's dead. He followed them back to their camp after he chatted with Hollis and Ryne—who I can't wait to see again, by the way." She clapped her hands in sudden excitement when she realized she had yet to see him. "But then he was gone the next day. I know where he is, but I haven't told anyone, don't worry." She looked to Lilith and gave her a strong nod as if they had discussed it previously.

"Thank you, Sunny. We appreciate that," Lilith responded. Brice was unsure if his mom really thought Sunny knew or if she was just playing along. Either way, he would ask his mom the truth of the matter later. Apparently, that was one more thing they didn't feel the need to discuss with him.

"Now what should we do?" Sunny asked, looking around the home again. She wandered into the kitchen area, trailing her hand along the backs of the chairs at the dining table.

"Since you are new to town, Sunny, we will have you meet with a group of people who are the leadership in town and get you registered as a guest," Lilith instructed.

"Speaking of registering, do you know how long you will be staying? And do the people you live with know where you are?" Aunt Letti asked in a nice way that sounded like regular conversation.

"I plan on living here! I want to go to school here. Macy told me about her school before she started to forget it, and it sounded fun. No one knows where I am. I just left. I come and go as I please usually. I did leave Grace a note that I was leaving and wouldn't be returning. I imagine she'll worry, but I think she knew the time was coming soon anyway." Sunny frowned. Brice wondered if talking about Grace or leaving upset her.

"Maybe you could send her a letter letting her know you're okay and with friends," Brice suggested, then amended at the scowl of her mother, "without telling them where you are, of course."

"That's a brilliant idea. Thank you, Brice. We're going to be good friends, you and I. I'm excited to go to school with you."

Brice blushed. He knew he did. He couldn't have stopped it if he had tried. "We'll have to get permission for you to attend for the remainder of the year."

He didn't think it was likely, but thought he'd shoot for the moon. It would be nice to have her at school. She was fun and pretty and it might be nice to have the fellas think he had a girlfriend for once. Not that she would be, of course.

"It will be fine. They let me go," she said as if it had already happened, which caught everyone off guard again.

"Sunny, how old are you?" Brice followed up to break the silence and to appease his own curiosity, "You know, so we can request to get you in the right grade."

"I'm sixteen." She paused and thought for a moment. "Well, I might be seventeen."

"They didn't know her exact birthdate when she came to live with us. So we guessed," Hollis answered before anyone asked.

"Ok, so probably a junior then," Brice offered as a safe bet.

Lilith sighed with exhaustion. "Well, let's start preparing for tacos, then we'll meet everyone at Court. The sooner we get this out in the open, the sooner we can figure out what comes next."

"It's not Tuesday, Mom," Brice stated. The Blackstones always had a family dinner for Taco Tuesday each week.

She stopped and stared out the window thoughtfully. "Tonight it's Tuesday. We're having tacos. Call your father and Brock. Hollis, Ryne is also invited. Aunt Letti, would you like to stay and invite Uncle Tranner too, please? Eva is on her way, so we'll make it a family gathering." Since Macy hadn't been able to make many of the family dinners, his mom had taken to inviting more of the extended family.

Brice shot Aunt Letti a look. His mom seemed a little off. They hadn't seen her like that in a long time. Brice gave Macy a look then a nod. He was concerned about his mom. Something in her facial expressions looked haunted.

"I'll call Dad," Brice offered, then shot out of the room to use the landline in the office. Cell coverage was spotty in the mountains unless you had a magically altered phone, which was reserved for the members of the Court and perhaps a select few others. But not Brice.

CHAPTER 6

The next day, Brice went back to school. The Academy started early, and he usually rode his skateboard if the weather allowed, as it wasn't that far from their house in Havenwood Heights, but Brice still felt drained from his restless nights, so he asked his dad if he'd drop him off. He'd struggled getting dressed with a sling over his arm. Thankfully, the doctor didn't deem it necessary for him to sport a full cast since he could heal faster with the witch's salve.

"Are you all right, son? You look a little pale," his father, Reggie, noted as they turned out of their aged but prestigious neighborhood of old money, passing through the iron gates and onto Blackstone Road —named after his ancestors who first arrived by wagon train in the 1850s with the other settlers of the town.

Brice appreciated his dad's concern. He turned himself sideways in the passenger seat to face his father. Reggie—Reginald to no one—was human, but his superpower was putting up with Brice's mom, at least in Brice's opinion. His dad was taller than him still and more muscular —but hopefully not for too much longer—and his hair was dark like his, but his eyes were a warm brown. To many others looking in from the outside, his dad was soft and let his mom walk all over him. But those who knew him knew that wasn't true. Reggie was strong and more than capable to handle a bunch of different situations including marrying into a family of witch hunters. He had climbed his way up the family business, and Brice's grandfather wouldn't have given Reggie all the responsibility he had just because he was in the family. Reggie had earned his place there, and he could handle Lilith Blackstone as well. His father just had a natural ability and temperament to come at things with a big-picture perspective that allowed him to come across as more relaxed. No one worked harder than his dad did—at least in Brice's opinion.

Brice considered his dad's question and decided to offer up some honesty. "I'm in pain from my wrist and not happy about having to wait out the healing without the witch's salve, but I understand why you and mom are holding it back. But I've been having strange dreams too, I think from the pain meds, so I haven't been sleeping much."

"She may not show it, Brice, but you scared your mother something fierce when she heard you had an accident and how bad it could've been. But I'll talk to her and see if we can get you that salve soon. As far as the dreams go, we can alter the prescription dosage if they're too strong, but what kind of dreams are you talking about?"

"Strange voices, someone talking to me, some electrical shows, and sometimes I think I can even feel little shocks from them . . . that kind of stuff." Brice shrugged, uncomfortable mentioning his private dreams.

"Interesting," his father started. "Keep me in the loop on that one and let me know if it keeps happening or changes, all right? And I'll talk to Dr. Underwood about lowering the dosage."

"Thanks, Dad." Brice gathered his backpack as his father turned right on First Street, then up to the guarded gates. Reggie rolled down his window and gave the morning guard a friendly salute as they passed through the tall gates. From there, it was a drive up a long stone road lined with trees on either side until the old stone mansion of a building loomed before them. The school was located on acres of pristine manicured lawns and stone pathways surrounded by stone walls to protect and guard it from humans. Multiple smaller buildings were set around the larger one. The entire school held more of a college-campus vibe than a high school. More traffic came and went than in years past; the portal to the Halvard Campus for the SMA college was located near the Falls Campus and students and faculty both used it. They came upon the school's main entrance, and the drive circled in front of the school for easy drop-off access. When there was an extra car to drive, Brice would park in the lot off to the left side.

"Have a good day, son," Reggie offered as Brice got out of the car.

"You, too, Dad. Hey, did you hear how the Court hearing with Sunny went last night? I wasn't allowed to go, and I couldn't stay awake to hear from Mom." He glanced to the side of the car and watched as another car pulled up behind them and let out some students who waved to Brice as they proceeded into school.

Reggie smiled. "I heard they are going to let her stay on a trial basis, truly in order to see why she might really be here. Elsmed Fairchild tested her, and she passed everything. But they are all there to be skeptical and protect the town, so they think she might have ulterior motives or at least be sent by someone, similar to the way Hollis arrived."

"She doesn't. Have other motives, I mean. I can just tell. There is an innocence to her that is disarming, don't you think?"

Reggie watched his son, then nodded. "She does indeed. Oh, also they are going to let her come to school, also on a trial basis. She should be here today as a junior, I think." Reggie knowingly smiled and waved his son off. "I have to get to work. See you afterward!"

Brice backed up and let his dad drive away as he waved.

"She might be here today?" he said quietly under his breath. Brice's heart rate sped up, and his feet felt like lead. He straightened his tie and shifted his blue blazer with the school crest on it to its proper place on his shoulders. Slowly he moved through the large arched entryway into the interior courtyard, the heart of the Academy. Brice didn't know if he should wait for her or not, but if he did wait much longer he'd miss first period. Since he didn't have classes with her anyway, he assumed Hollis would be bringing her and would help her get settled, so he went ahead to homeroom so he wouldn't be late.

His morning classes passed in a blur; he could barely remember

what was assigned for homework. Too much was on his mind. At lunch he sat with some of the guys he'd skated with and gave a wave to Cade Peters at another table. He also saw one of the twins, Remy MacKinnon—but Remy didn't want to be there, if his expression said anything about it. Maybe he just didn't want to be there without his twin, Roxy, who was allowed to skip senior year and go to the college of guardians a year early. The dining hall, as well as administrative offices and old original classrooms, were located in the Founder's Hall, one of three wings of the Academy. But Brice's favorite room, contrary to what many would suspect, was the Havenwood House Book and Manuscript Library. The Academy was old but well maintained, beautiful, and held a magic all its own. Brice loved it.

Without warning, he felt a buzzing, more like a low-level itch at the back of his neck. He scratched at it, but nothing was there. He scratched a second time until he realized the tingles at the base of his neck meant another witch hunter was nearby; only he had never felt it before. His head shot from one side to the other, scanning each end of the lunchroom for the source of his discomfort, until he saw her.

Sunny had made it to school.

CHAPTER 7

The interior of the dining hall was large and medieval looking, constructed of large gray stones with vaulted ceilings. Long, wooden tables a century old stretched in multiple rows from one end of the room to the other. Brice knew a kitchen existed, but he had yet to see the proof. The room, and entire hall, essentially looked like the interior of a Gothic castle but with modern updates to accommodate the school. The electrical system had been updated, but still the sconces appeared as if they had fire burning in them, complete with flickers of light playing with shadow against the stones for effect. Other parts of the school were more modern, especially Memorial Hall, but Brice liked the old-world feel of the older parts of the Academy.

Sunny made a beeline straight for Brice without even needing the time to look for him. He had to admit she looked pretty cute in her navy blue blazer, crisp white shirt, and blue skirt with knee-high dress socks and shoes. With the dining hall filled with people and their chaotic noises like it was, he was surprised she found him so quickly. Though if he could feel her just barely with his hunter gifts awakening, she could probably pin him down like a needle in a haystack since she had grown up with her abilities and learned how to use them long ago.

He understood and even agreed with why the town and his family placed restrictions on them until they were older, but it sure would be nice to already have full access to whatever he was going to be able to do.

His heart sped up as she moved closer, though she took her time absorbing the surroundings of the room. He realized she was much more observant than she let on. Brice didn't know if she put on an act with the whimsical, almost oblivious, way she seemed to move through life or if she somehow processed life a little differently than most. Her blond hair, fair complexion, and overall shininess was a pure juxtaposition to the doom and gloom of the architecture.

And he wasn't the only one to notice. A hush fell over the room, and many stared. Brice suddenly felt uncomfortable with how they stared at her, knowing she was on her way toward him. He had enough trouble with standing out. He hadn't thought through what her presence might actually mean for him. He had hoped for the benefits of her arrival, but now considered there might be drawbacks as well. A catcall and a few whistles reverberated from the back of the hall. Sunny didn't seem to notice or care, but Brice was shocked at the instantaneous surge of jealousy and anger that rushed through his body. She wasn't his. She didn't belong to him. He barely even knew her, but something inside him said otherwise. He stood from his seat and shot a glare at the offender who, of course, happened to be Chadwick Linton. So surprised at his sudden action, he didn't notice the tiny sparks that shot from his fingertips when he did so.

Sunny came right up alongside him and placed her small, delicate hand around his elbow.

"Hello, Brice! See, I get to come to school with you." She went on as if she hadn't noticed anything about the altercation about to happen right in front of her eyes. Perhaps she didn't, or perhaps she knew just what to do to quickly defuse the situation.

Brice deflated and looked at her. Something in her eyes brought peace to his soul, and he gave her a quick nod, inhaling through his nose to calm his adrenaline-filled body.

"Great . . . really, that's great news, Sunny." Brice brought his train

31

of thought on track to where she had directed. "Hey, do you want to see some of the campus before our next classes?"

Sunny's face beamed, and she nodded with excitement. "Please!"

Brice showed her around the Founder's Hall they were already in, then moved to the other two wings.

"This wing we are entering is Memorial Hall. It has more of the newer and more modern classrooms in it. Which is pretty cool, if you like that sort of style." He glanced over at Sunny to find her eyes wide, soaking in all the details.

"Show me more, Brice! There is so much to see," Sunny said with a huge smile.

"Okay, this next wing is the Falls Campus. You'll find classes for supernatural training at Castor Center in this wing, as well as sports fields and access points to areas around the falls."

They walked in silence for several more minutes as they circled their way back to Founder's Hall, ending at his favorite room: the library.

"This is the best room in the entire Academy—at least that's what I think," Brice said as he opened the door and smiled. "This is the Havenwood House Book and Manuscript Library."

Sunny gasped and practically squealed as she did. Bouncing on the balls of her feet, she innocently asked, "Are we allowed to go in?"

"Of course," Brice said and ushered her in.

"I love libraries. Dante always chose my books for me, but I love to read." She twirled as she stepped completely inside. "This is like a world I want to live in."

Brice smiled and simply watched her enjoy one of his favorite spaces. Even when he was a student at Havenwood Falls High, he enjoyed coming to this library for evening classes or whenever he could. The afternoon light flooded the room with a warm glow through the wall of stained glass windows, overlaying the colors along the wood beams bracing the room for the incredible dome at its center. The dome was a work of art depicting supernatural creatures of all kinds throughout the ages and lent to the sacred feel of the library. The room was spacious in the middle, but lined with two stories of mahogany shelves filled with books from ancient leather-bound tomes to modern works of fiction and nonfiction alike. Brice followed Sunny as she moved as if guided by the wind through the mahogany tables carved with beautiful detail.

"Can you feel it?" Sunny asked with a reverent whisper.

"Feel what?"

"The presence. The history. The weight of knowledge. The magic. It's all in this room." She held out her arms, taking it all in.

Brice thoughtfully considered what she said and extended his senses, trying to feel what she felt.

"I'm not sure I feel it, but maybe I do, and that's why I love this room." He shrugged, uncertain what else to say.

"You'll feel it all in time," she said with a smile and pranced over to one of the shelves. With a featherlight touch, she brushed her fingers along several of the spines as she read them.

"You talk as if you know things already."

She stopped and turned to look at him. Her eyes shone, and her face reflected some of the reds and oranges from the stained glass. She smiled then and said, "I do. But don't tell anyone else."

Sunny winked at him and returned to her perusal of the shelf.

Brice paused. "Why do you think you know what's going to happen?"

"Because the voices tell me. Well, sometimes they show me pictures," she told him, as if what she said was everyday conversation.

Brice was surprised to hear she had voices in her head. Maybe she was on meds, too. Or maybe if his voices didn't go away, she could help him figure out what to do about it. He hoped that wasn't the case, though.

"Sunny? Can I ask you about your voices?"

"Yes, but you need to know they are a part of me. I know them. They've been with me all my life, unlike yours. Your voice is new. Your voice is hiding. Be careful, Brice. Your voice is giving me a headache," she said suddenly with a groan, as her hand went to hold the top of her head.

Brice rushed over to her and put his hand under her elbow,

guiding her to one of the bench seats under a window pane. "Sunny, are you okay? Should I get someone?"

He looked around. They were the only ones in the library, as it was still lunch time. He started to get up, but she pulled him down to sit next to her.

"No. Not yet. It's magic, and it's blocking me for some reason. Just give me a second. It will pass," Sunny said quietly as she focused on her breathing.

Brice realized he had never felt so helpless to do anything for someone. He realized he cared. After a moment, Sunny inhaled slowly and opened her eyes, releasing her head.

"It's over." She stood up and pulled Brice up with her, his hand in hers. "Thank you for sitting with me. No one has done that for me before. It's nice." Without any other words, she let go of his hand and made her way all around the room, studying everything. Brice stayed where he was, unsure what had just happened.

"Sunny, are you sure you're okay?" he asked, concerned. Nervously, he put one hand in a pocket, and the other kept swiping at the shock of hair continuing to fall into his eyes.

Sunny skipped over to him. "I am sure. It will stop soon enough, just a little longer."

"Are you a fortune teller?" Brice skeptically asked.

She cocked her head in confusion at him, but then added a small smile. "What do you think?"

"Um, no?" he ventured uncertainly.

"You will just have to wait until after school, because I need to get to my next class. Bye, Brice!" she said with a friendly wave and swiftly blew out of the room as if ushered by the same wind that guided her in.

Brice shook his head. "That was weird. She is . . . I don't know what she is. She's something special for sure and maybe something more."

Remembering how he felt in the dining hall when the other boys had jeered at Sunny, he wanted to see if he could find any information regarding witch hunters or strange occurrences during awakenings. In

fact, he could have asked Sunny, and maybe he should have. He would have to remember to ask her after school. She had to have seen the sparks and known it was part of the reawakening, or she chose to ignore it. He had some study time before his last class, and he would spend it there, researching anything he could find. Being a senior, he had a little more free time, plus the campus functioned more like a college, allowing the students to study independently when not in class. He just hoped he could find something to help him or he'd have to ask his mom. That was a conversation he didn't want to have yet.

CHAPTER 8

*B*rice searched for what felt like hours and countless tomes with no luck of any information that would help him find answers. Out of frustration, he laid his head down on the table.

"Brice? Can you hear me?" The same voice from his dreams spoke to him, but this time he could tell it was male. Brice's head shot off the table, and he looked around frantically for the source.

"Who's there? Where are you?" he answered out loud.

"Brice, I can sense you are beginning to allow your hunter to reawaken."

"You can? How can you know that? Are you spying on me?" He quietly tiptoed around the room, grateful he didn't find anyone, but at the same time unnerved because someone was speaking into his mind.

"Let's just say I have my ways and leave it at that."

"What do you want? Why are you bothering me?" Brice asked, starting to get frustrated.

"I do not intend to bother you. I intend to help you. Your family does not have time to fully help you through your transition. They haven't been completely honest with you."

"What do you mean?" Brice had a sinking feeling, most likely because he'd had that thought before, and having it confirmed by a bodiless stranger hurt.

"I think you know. Ask your mother about the family journal and the dagger."

And just like that, the voice was silent. Brice's heart raced. He tried to calm himself down. The voice said it intended to help him. He didn't trust a random voice, but maybe it was his guardian angel. He knew people who actually had those. Might be cool if he had his own too. Once he was calm, he thought the advice might be sound. It might be wise for him to dig more into his family history. He knew the rogue Blackstones had several male witch hunters. There had to be a record of why somewhere.

Brice looked at the clock on his phone and realized he had to hurry.

It felt like forever, but in reality he had only used up his study period, and he had one more class before the end of the day to get to. Still slightly shaken, he put away the books he had pulled down to a table and cleaned up the space he used. He rolled his neck and stretched his arms. The tingles shot through his forearms again, and his skin felt like it was crawling. He had to get ahold of himself and shake off the agitation; he felt like he needed to run laps or something.

The door opened and in walked Ronya Augustine, Gallad's mom and Macy's future mother-in-law. Gallad and Macy had gotten engaged earlier in the year but decided to make it an extended engagement so they could both attend SMA.

"Hello, Brice. Catching up on some studying?" Ronya said with a cheerful smile as she carted a box into the room. Brice felt a low-level zing up his arms as she entered. He flexed his fingers and shook out his hands, not used to the sensation, hopefully before she saw him.

"Oh, just a little research . . . hold on, let me help you with that." Brice ran over to her just in time. He grabbed the box awkwardly with a broken wrist right before she dropped it.

"Oh, my hero. Thank you, Brice. I thought I could get it all in one trip, but apparently I should have made two." She placed her purse and another bag onto one of the tables and directed him to set the box there too. Brice realized the box was lighter than when he first grabbed it and felt a zing of power under his wrist. Ronya was using magic to help him help her. He would have been embarrassed except it really helped and he thought it was pretty cool. She winked at him and held her finger to her lips. "Shh, don't tell."

"I know nothing." He smiled, then gestured to the box. "Is this for your class tonight?"

Brice knew Ronya—or Mrs. Augustine—taught the Awakening Lab for supernaturals learning their powers after hours. Her son, Gallad, also assisted with supernatural histories class in the evenings, but since he enrolled with SMA Gallad's involvement was limited.

"Yes, I'm a little early, aren't I?" she said with a wink. He liked Ronya. She had a sunny personality. That thought instantly sent his thoughts toward Sunny herself.

He hoped Sunny was enjoying her classes and wished he could be there to watch her. Her fascination with all things was oddly refreshing.

Oblivious to the wandering of Brice's mind, Ronya continued talking. "I am grabbing some books, then meeting Gallad here after his classes. And I'll have him help me get this box over to the Falls Campus for class tonight."

"How is Gallad liking SMA? Macy is pretty cryptic about it all," Brice said to be conversational.

Ronya stopped and looked at him conspiratorially. "Gallad is the same way. He says it's hard, but deep down I think he loves it. He has always liked a good academic challenge, no matter what kind of image he was trying to portray. That's one thing I love about your sister—she understands that about him, and she likes to learn, too, which I admire." She smiled. "But you don't need to know that, do you? He also said he's having a blast with all the new people the school has enrolled . . . supernaturals from all over. But we probably won't see too much of them in Havenwood Falls, considering they are there in secret, right?" She giggled to herself as she pulled item after item out of the box.

"True. I hope to check it out when they have hopefuls apply for next year. Seems like a cool thing to do."

Ronya looked up at him and then she looked around him as if sensing something amiss. "Brice? Are you alone here?"

She slowly scanned the room.

"Yes, I've been reading for the last hour. Why?"

She pursed her lips, then shook her head as if lost in thought. "No reason, I guess. There's just a negative energy residue, like something was here but then not really. It makes no sense. Never mind."

Brice was shocked at her keen sense of the supernatural. He didn't know if his voice was negative or not yet, but perhaps Ronya would be someone he could talk to.

"Mrs. Augustine, I don't have much time before my next class, but could I ask you questions sometime about awakenings?"

"Of course you can, Brice." She walked over next to him and placed her hand on his shoulder. She joined him as he moved toward the door. "However, I think your family would be best suited for witch hunter awakenings, if you think that's what's going on."

"No, it's actually for a friend. He isn't from a witch family but has been experiencing some strange things, and he doesn't know who to ask or what's going on with him. I told him I'd ask around."

Ronya glanced at Brice, but to him, it felt like she peered into the depths of his soul, reading everything about him he didn't want anyone to know. Of course, she wasn't, but still.

"You tell your friend I'd be happy to help anyway I can. He could come to one of the Awakening Lab classes, too. That might help. Or you could come with him or for him, if he didn't want to be outed just yet, and take notes," she offered with such grace and ease, he almost agreed right then. "The class takes place in Castor Center."

"Thanks, Mrs. Augustine. I'll let him know. And maybe I will try to get him to come to the class tonight. Gotta go. Talk to you later!"

"See you at class, Brice." Ronya waved to him with a knowing but friendly smile.

CHAPTER 9

*A*fter school, Brice waited outside in the courtyard for Sunny. His brother, Brock, had pulled into the parking lot in their grandfather's old pickup truck, meaning he was working at the vineyard, and waved to him out his rolled-down window. Brice held up his finger signaling for Brock to wait a minute. Brock saluted then turned up his music and leaned his head back against the seat.

After another minute, Sunny came bounding out from the courtyard through the large archway with a smile on her face and her hair bouncing along with her.

"Hey, Brice! I've had the best day. School is amazing."

"Hey, Sunny, was everyone nice to you? Did you find your classes okay?" Brice asked, concerned.

"I don't worry about other people so much, but the ones I talked with were friendly. Did you know there are all kinds of supernaturals that go here?" She lowered her voice as if it were a secret.

"I did know. They go to the public school, Havenwood Falls High, too. Here they can be more open about who they are and what they can do. But they can't at the public school because there are unknowing humans that go there, too."

"So the humans can't go here. That would explain why I didn't see any," she said absently.

Brice cleared his throat. "Sunny, do you have plans for today? I was wondering if you would like to visit the great falls, then my family's vineyard—well, I have to check in there anyway after school, but we could take a detour."

Sunny smiled and clapped her hands together. "Yes, I would love to see the waterfall. Hollis told me to go home with you however you got there after school. So that's what we shall do, then."

"My brother, Brock, is right over there to drive us."

"I haven't met him yet." She followed him to the truck and Brock got out.

"Hey, Brice. And you must be Sunny. I'm Brock—the big brother." He stuck out his chest proudly. "Hollis told me to be on the lookout for you," Brock said.

Without warning, Sunny grabbed Brock around the middle in a big hug, catching both guys off guard. Brock awkwardly shrugged at Brice who felt like he had been punched in the gut. She hadn't welcomed him like that. "I've always wanted a big brother. The boys at my other home were . . . not who I wanted for a brother."

"But this guy will work?" Brice questioned, then laughed when Brock lightly socked him in the stomach.

"Yes, he is perfect." Sunny stepped back. "Brice mentioned you might able to take us to the great waterfall. I'd really love to see it."

"How can a brother say no to that face?" Brock said and ushered her around to the passenger side of the truck, gallantly opening the door for her to slide in. He looked at Brice, who was at a loss and simply laughed.

"To the falls, good man." Brice joined in the fun.

The falls weren't that far from the Academy, but they had to go back out to Blackstone Road and turn up a couple blocks later on Alverson Road.

"It is really special you have a road named after you," Sunny noted as they turned off it.

"Well, in truth, it's named after our ancestors who came with the first settlers to establish this town over one hundred fifty years ago,"

Brock explained, as he drove up the road that would lead to the trails into the falls.

"Having history is important. I admire that you have that." Sunny seemed to drift into a daze, then looked at Brice with a vacant expression. "You should understand Judson more."

Brice and Brock exchanged a quick look. Brice was confused. "How do you know about Judson?"

She came back to her bright self and lowered her head as if to tell him a secret and tapped her head. "The voices, remember?"

"Do you mean Judson Blackstone? He was the husband of Marie Blackstone. They were the ancestors I just mentioned," Brock said with fascination. He found the timing wild, as he had just been in the library looking for information on his family history.

"Yes, that sounds right," she said.

The rest of the ride remained quiet until Brock pulled them into an area at the trailhead. "This is your stop, m'lady."

Brice opened the door and helped her out. "Will you tell Dad, or whoever is at the vineyard today, I'll be late but we'll be there after I show Sunny the falls?"

Brock nodded.

"Thank you, kind sir, for safe passage," Sunny said in her most formal tone and did an elaborate curtsy for Brock.

He howled and blew her a kiss. "I like this one!"

Brice rolled his eyes. Then Brock drove away. He knew his brother was harmless and most likely why he didn't feel the same surge of jealousy he had at school when the others paid attention to Sunny. With his brother, they were safe.

"I like him, too!" Sunny joyfully declared. "Yes, he will make the perfect brother."

"Yeah, he's pretty cool," Brice agreed. "Follow me. I'll show you something else pretty cool."

They walked up one of the trails, and as they got closer, Sunny gasped before they even saw the water. "I can feel it. It's magical."

She took a deep breath and let the mist rolling through the forest wash over her.

Brice watched her with awe. He had never met anyone like her before. She was so open and free—he longed for that feeling. "What's it feel like?"

She smiled with her eyes closed. "It's refreshing and reenergizing. The magic tingles along my skin. That's the hunter in me, that I can sense it so strong. I can also feel there are witch wards around it—many of them, for different reasons."

Brice was shocked. "I've never heard of a hunter who could decipher magical wards—sense them maybe, but not that strong."

"I'm not like all hunters, Brice. In case you haven't noticed."

"You know you're not like the others?" Brice was hesitant to ask, but since she opened the door he was curious.

"Yes, I know. I've always known. Dante tried to make me like the others but soon realized I couldn't be, because I'm not."

They continued to walk in a little farther. He really wanted to see her reaction when she actually saw the water. Rushing water splashed as it hit the pool at the base of the falls. Brice helped her over some rough terrain as they emerged from the trees into a small clearing made only for the falls. The water at the base was shimmering at the reflection of the sun and surrounded by large boulders and an explosion of foliage.

"Wow," Sunny breathed with awe. She appeared speechless as she fully took the sight in. "This sight alone is magic. Can I live here?"

Brice chuckled. "I don't think so."

"How tall is the waterfall?"

"From my history book . . . I think about three hundred feet high."

"And the water is magical?" she said more as a statement than a question, but since no one was supposed to know that, he took it as a question.

"Well, most don't know that, but yes, it has magical properties," he explained. "But you can't tell anyone that, okay?" he added, suddenly wondering if he was supposed to be showing her secrets of the town.

"I don't plan on going anywhere, Brice," she stated honestly. "Your Court will end up liking me, and I'll get to stay."

"Sunny? Is Dante your father?" Brice ripped off the Band-Aid and just asked what was on his mind.

CHAPTER 10

*S*unny giggled, then quickly sobered. "No. Many think that. He made many people think that, but no, he is not. I think he took me from them."

Brice frowned. "Took you from who?"

"My parents. I don't remember them. I was young, but I have flashes of them in my dreams."

Brice was in way over his head. Should he hug her? Hold her hand? "Even if he didn't, I'm sorry you didn't have them in your life. What do you think happened to them?"

"I miss who they could've been. He told me they died in a fire when I was about three or four. I think he killed them."

Brice reared his head back. She spoke so casually of the situation, but for her, he reminded himself, it was so long ago, and she didn't remember them.

"Why would he do that, Sunny? I mean, I know he didn't care for witches and killed a lot of them, but why would he do that to his own people?" Brice asked, genuinely confused.

"From what little I've learned, my mother was a powerful witch hunter, but my father was a Seer—and that, to Dante, was too close to a witch. He hated him, but Dante let them stick around after having me. He was curious what I would become. There had never been a witch hunter with seer abilities before."

"Does that mean you can tell the future?"

"No. Well, kinda. I *see* things. They don't always make sense, and I told you I hear voices—the voices are my family, the seers who have gone before me. They help me to decipher and understand things I see."

Brice was surprised at her honesty and seriousness.

"Dante thought he could use me to find you all, and predict how well his witch hunting raids would go. My gift doesn't work on demand, though. He tried to find ways to make it work for him, but he ultimately found if he just let me be, I'd cooperate." She snickered a little, then whispered as if Dante was within earshot, "I only gave him some information. And I never told him where your family was."

"So you gave him little nuggets and he left you alone?" Brice asked.

"Yep." She smiled again like she held the secrets of the world in her hand and she controlled how much got out, which he guessed she kind of did.

"And that's how you found your way here, to Havenwood Falls?"

She nodded. "I saw where the bus would be, and the driver did the rest!"

"Handy," Brice acknowledged.

"I saw you, too," she said with a smile.

"You did? Doing what?" Brice was a little concerned with what she might have seen. He didn't know what kinds of things her ancestors showed her, but he hoped he was portrayed in a good light.

"I saw you skateboarding just like you did the other day. So I knew where to find you."

He breathed a sigh of relief. He at least thought he looked cool when he rode his board.

"I also saw us at school . . . and then later together dancing. I don't know how to dance, though, so I thought that one was iffy." She shrugged as if it was no big deal she just told him they might be on a date together. "Sometimes the visions don't always work out how I see them, but mostly they do."

Brice's mouth went dry. He didn't know what kind of dancing they might do. They'd already missed homecoming at Havenwood Falls High by only a couple weeks. The Cold Moon Ball was still coming up in December, or maybe it was further away in the future. His heart raced, and his palms grew sweaty.

"Brice, don't worry about it. You have time—I think. I don't know exactly when the dance is, but it will be great when it's time." She smiled and moved toward the water's edge. She knelt down and dipped her fingers into the cool sparkling water and laughed.

He ran up next to her and kneeled on the ground.

"What is it?" He couldn't see anything out of the ordinary.

"The water tickles my skin. It's inviting me to play. Try it!" She playfully fluttered her fingers in a tickling motion within the water.

Brice awkwardly pushed his good hand into the water, but he didn't feel anything but cold, wet water. "I don't feel anything."

"You're trying too hard. Here, let me show you." She grabbed his hand in the water and pried open his tight fist, extending each of his fingers. She placed her hand against his, palm to palm and finger to finger. She slid each of her fingers loosely between his then moved his hand back and forth in the water.

Brice tried to remember how to breathe. He thought his heart was going to thump right out of his chest. He had never held hands with a girl—aside from the occasional assist to a girl by steadying her hand or you know, his family—not like that. She was so innocent, he was sure she meant nothing by it other than to help him, but in that moment, he wanted her to mean it. He wanted her to want him. He felt close to her, like he belonged, like he was seen for who he was and not just what he would be like when his hunter gifts reawakened.

"Can you feel it, Brice? Close your eyes and simply feel the water. Feel the magic in the water as it touches your skin." Her voice was calm and sweet and without any pressure.

Brice closed his eyes and slowly inhaled through his nose, working on steadying his breathing and racing heart as he did. He concentrated on the water, how it felt viscous and cool against his hand. He thought of the magic that flowed through the waters, providing the town and witches with a steady source of natural magical energy. Brice pictured that magic touching his skin and the water seeping into his pores, then crawling up his hand to his wrist, then encapsulating his forearm.

Sunny gasped with glee. "You did it!"

Brice opened his eyes to see water actually surrounding his arm—the water somehow did what he pictured and climbed his arm.

"How . . . how . . . I don't understand. How did the water do that?" Brice couldn't take his eyes off the water, then realized he was still holding Sunny's hand and quickly let go, breaking the spell, and the water splashed back into the pond.

"I did not see that. Brice, you have magic. Maybe that was why you always looked like you had mini fireworks around you when I saw you in visions." Sunny trailed off in thought, oblivious to Brice's near meltdown.

"Magic . . . I don't have magic," Brice mumbled as he stepped away from the falls. "How could I have magic? I'm a witch hunter—at least, I'm supposed to be." He looked at his hands. Tiny electrical arcs moved around the surface of his hands while simultaneously shocks formed at the base of his wrists and shot up his forearms all the way to his shoulders. He flexed his fingers, then shook his hands.

Shook his hands. Brice looked down at both hands and then solely at the right one. He could move his wrist without pain. "I can move my wrist! My wrist is healed." He rotated it again with more awe than he had the first time. "How is this possible?"

Sunny scrunched her face up, then her eyes widened.

"Well, if you have magic, you're a witch. You healed yourself with your witch magic," she concluded, as if it was completely obvious.

"Except I'm not a witch. How would I be a witch? Everyone in my family is witch hunter, human, or something else other than a witch. Gallad's the only witch who will be in our family, but he's not blood, and they don't have children yet. I wonder what will happen when they have kids?" Brice rambled as he continued to back away from the falls in a bit of a confused stupor. "I can't be a witch. I just thought I might be having a different kind of awakening."

"You are!" Sunny jumped in with excitement. "You're awakening both a witch and a hunter." She instantly frowned. "Well, that's why your body is so confused. You must be fighting against yourself. Interesting."

Brice shook out his hands, alleviating the electrical charges. "We need to go. My parents will wonder what's taking so long." He paused and looked at Sunny. "Hey, will you not tell my parents or anyone about all this yet? I want some time to process whatever this is that's happening." He looked to see his hands once more to ensure they were free of any evidence of magic and that his wrist was still healed. "Maybe I should put my brace back on, too, until I know why it happened."

"Okay. You'll be okay, Brice. I can't wait to see the vineyard," she said, as if none of the previous events bothered her in the slightest. They simply were the way they were meant to be.

Brice wished he could accept whatever it was that easily, but he felt sick to his stomach. Maybe he would go to Ronya's class after all.

CHAPTER 11

*A*t their visit to the vineyard, Brice introduced Sunny to several workers and to his Uncle Tranner, who happened to be there picking up Aunt Letti for the evening. He showed her around the vines, where they made the wine, the bar area, and NamaStays Inn with all its small cabins they rented out to visitors. She seemed particularly interested in the Yoga in the Vines classes and wondered if she could attend one. She and Aunt Letti made plans for her to come back with Hollis to take a class one morning before school the next week. Sunny loved everything about the vineyard and made everyone she encountered smile. Brice envied the ease and simplicity with which she saw life, even though what she truly saw had to have been anything but simple. He thought on that while he and his dad prepared the barbecue and food for dinner that night at the vineyard. Hollis and Sunny had left, saying they had plans for dinner to meet Ryne and his mom, Jessica Calloway.

Macy was still at school and not coming home, so it was just Brock, his mom and dad, and his grandma Eva who stayed for dinner. His mom and grandma set the table on the patio in front of the bar area. The winery was still open, but it was a slow night, so the few people who lingered sat on bar stools inside, chatting it up with Brock while he wiped down the counters. Brice moved over to where Brock was working when he finished helping his dad and looked out the windows of the modern garage doors, now closed as the evening air grew chillier and chillier. The patio area was filled with small table sets surrounding one big wooden table with bench seats and interwoven with barrels for personal fires. Over their heads was a fun canopy of strung Edison lights.

"Need any help in here, Brock?" Brice asked his brother just as he finished the last table.

"Nope, I think I'm done. You timed it just right." Brock snapped the dish towel he had at the back of Brice's legs, causing him to jump out of the way before he remembered to clutch his arm as if it had caused him pain. "Oh shoot, Brice, I'm sorry. Forgot about your arm."

"It's okay. It's not as bad as it was." Brice absently rubbed his wrist, thinking of what had happened at the falls earlier.

"You all right, man? You seem kind of out of it tonight," Brock intuitively observed.

"Yeah, I'm okay." Brice picked up a couple random glasses Brock had gathered onto one table and started to take them into the kitchen area. "How are your micros?" Brice asked, referring to the microbrews Brock had been testing out in the cellar until his operation got too big and had to move into the out building where they made the wine.

Brock gave Brice a big cocky smile. "I think they are doing awesome! You gotta try some of 'em out, little brother. I just need you to get a little older."

"Dude, we own a winery. I've tasted the wine we sell."

"There's that." Brock nodded his concession.

"I was thinking, maybe in the future it would be cool to work together with the micros—I love making 'em with you already. It could be fun!"

Brock really looked at Brice like he had never thought of that idea before. He seemed to be considering the idea then suddenly smiled. "I like it! Finish school, then we'll talk, but I'll keep it in my mind. Mom and Dad need to take on a few more employees here anyway since Macy went back to school. Maybe they could look for a couple more to give me a little more time, so we can plan for it.

"It could be a division of the winery or Soothing Sips. We could call it *Blackstone Brothers* or *The Blackstone Brothers Brewery*. The name has a nice ring to it, don't you think?" Brice asked, suddenly self-conscious about his idea and name until Brock smiled again. This time his smile touched the edges of his eyes, and he knew he had him.

"It's perfect. I'll start working on a logo. I was trying to think of how to brand the micros. You just solved it. Good job, little brother." Brock reached over and shook Brice's hand. "Future partners?"

Brice smiled and shook his hand in return. "Partners."

"All right, boys, food is ready. Come and eat!" their grandma called through the door from outside. She was a tall and regal woman with her hair cut into a short, sharp bob and a fierce attitude not unlike the one she must have passed on to her daughter.

They all gathered around one end of the large wood table now filled with plates of steak, hamburgers, and chicken. There were also bowls of various salads, both green and pasta, as well as platters of fruit. They entertained small talk while they ate and even visited with the last of the customers as they came to say their goodbyes. The fall nights were quite chilly up in the mountain, but the barrels of fire kept heat radiating close enough to keep them warm. At the end of their meal they sat and sipped on coffee or wine as twilight replaced daylight after the sun had descended behind Miles Mountain.

"Brice, your mother and I have decided to give you the witch's salve to speed up the rest of your recovery," his father said, passing him a small box filled with what he knew was a healing balm for his already healed wrist. They didn't know that, however, so he took the box.

"Thank you," Brice said.

"How did Sunny do at her first day of school?" Lilith asked dryly.

Brice could tell his mom was not thrilled to have Sunny in town. He didn't know if she didn't trust the girl's intentions even though she passed Elsmed's test or if she didn't like that others from the rogue group were infringing upon her self-importance in the little town, and bringing with them possible new ways of being a witch hunter—still without doing the hunting part.

"I think she did okay," Brice answered. "She was talking with some girls when I saw her outside one of her classes. I gave her a short tour of Founder's Hall, then she had to go to her own classes. I spoke with Ronya a little too. She was setting up for her class tonight, and she invited me to come check it out as my hunter abilities will be showing up soon."

"That was thoughtful of her, son, but she knows very little about the witch hunters, being a witch herself," his mother said absently as if lost in another thought, not fully engaged with the conversation she began herself. She then looked up at him. "But you aren't experiencing any more symptoms yet, are you," she said as more of a statement, though that bothered Brice because she didn't even truly ask or maybe she didn't even want to know. So he wouldn't tell her.

"Hey, Grandma? Can you tell me more about Marie and Judson Blackstone? I was looking in the library for any mention of them since they were some of the town founders. I wanted to learn more of our history, but couldn't find much."

She pursed her lips at first then nodded to Lilith, who turned her head away and looked up at the mountain.

"Is it a secret or something?" Brice asked hesitantly.

"No, no, boy, it was just a very long time ago. Their history is mostly passed down through stories, and I suppose it's time to share them with you. It would be convenient if your sister were here, as well. She learned some of it at her orientation for her reawakening, just as you will. But tonight is as good a time as any."

Brice was interested to learn more of his history. He didn't understand why they made it such a big deal to share it when they were approaching their reawakening, but maybe he'd finally find out.

"Their history takes place in the mid-1800s on the East Coast in Virginia. The Blackstones were an affluent family of tobacco farmers who ventured into grape cultivating for the wine business. The matriarch of the home was Cessily Blackstone, who was also an ambassador and friend to the neighboring village of witches called the Stronghold Coven. Marie, the youngest, wanted to follow in her mother's path after she died, but Dante, her brother, wanted the power of being the witch hunter he felt they had the right to be. Marie's best friend was the daughter of the coven leader, and her secret husband, Judson, who was human, was raised by the witches. Dante didn't like it, and he rallied the other siblings and relatives who had the hunter gene to rise up and take the birthright he felt they were owed. He hated that Marie was—as he called it—blinded to the truth of who they were and that she associated with the witches even after their mother had gone. He burned down the Stronghold Coven's village, killing many of the witches, including the leader. Marie, their father, and several others, including a handful of the coven, fled Virginia and headed west on a wagon train that ultimately met up with the other founders such as the early—and some current—Beaumonts, Bishops, Augustines, Fairchilds, Mills, Stuarts, and our Marie and Judson." His grandma paused and took a drink of her wine and a much needed break from speaking.

"So Dante has been pursuing Marie and her descendants this whole time?" Brice asked with dumbfounded awe. "Why?"

"He believed if he could find Marie and take away all her outlets for her dream to find a new life and way of living as a witch hunter, she would see the error of her ways and come back to him, the family, and their way of life. He felt it was his job to make sure they were all where they were *supposed to be*," his father added with air quotes.

"That's absurd, it doesn't even make that much sense."

"To him it did," Lilith quietly said. "He was very persuasive."

Brice watched his mom. "Did you know him?"

Her gaze found his, and the flatness he saw there told him she had and wished she hadn't.

"It was quite some time ago." Her tone suggested she wouldn't say more on the issue.

"Does anyone know where he is now?" Brice asked, his eyes darting from each member of his family. It was quiet for an awkward moment.

"He's in the Infernum, Brice," his mom finally answered.

CHAPTER 12

"He's in the Infernum, and nobody said anything?" Brice stood from his seat. The Infernum was a part of Hell reserved for supernaturals. "That's kind of a big deal, don't you think? He's been searching for us for years. Does Macy know?"

His mother looked down for a fraction of a second.

"She knows," Brice guessed. "Does everyone know but me?"

"No, it's been kept quiet around the town. We detained him last May after he confronted Hollis. Her truth hit him more than he would let on, and he made a mistake, allowing us to follow him. We were ready, and with the help of Uncle Tranner, Roman Bishop, and Saundra Beaumont, we were able to capture him. He's now and forever secured in the Infernum."

"It's good he's out of the picture, but why not tell me?" He sat back down in a slump.

"Because there was no reason to," his mom answered, then added, "and the less information you have about him, the better."

Brice reared back as if she had slapped him. "Why?"

No one said anything, but eyes drifted toward Lilith. Finally she answered, "Because I don't want you to have anything to do with him."

She slowly stood and went into the bar area to grab another bottle of wine.

"Fine," grumbled Brice. "I'll let it go for now. But I'm sick of being in the dark all the time." He inhaled a deep breath and sipped on his coffee, then looked to his grandma while his dad and Brock cleared the table. "Can you tell me anything else about Judson?"

His grandma cocked her head and stared at him. "Why the sudden interest in him?"

Brice shrugged. "I heard his named mentioned, and I realized I should know more about my great-great-grandfather."

"Sunny," his mom breathed with frustration as she sat back down at the table. "This is Sunny's doing, isn't it?"

Brice didn't say anything. He didn't want to bring Sunny into their discussion.

"I'm just curious," he said with more conviction.

"Well, I know some, but without knowing what you're looking for, I'm not sure what to tell you about him. I got my information handed down from my mother," his grandma said. She bit the inside of her lip and shot a glance at Lilith.

"There may be a way to find out more . . ." his grandma hesitated.

"Mother," Lilith said with a warning in her tone, "it hasn't been found in generations."

"The kids have a right to know about it. Plus, he might be able to find it," she shot back in their secret code speak.

"He's not ready yet."

Eva looked Brice over from top to bottom and nodded. "I think he's ready."

Brice's head bobbed back and forth between the two as if watching a tennis match. "Ready for what?"

"Marie had a journal from her ancestors that is rumored to hold all the knowledge of the witch hunters from our past. It was supposedly hidden, and no one has found it," his grandmother explained. "We searched all the places we could think of, but at some point, we stopped searching."

"A journal? What else could it hold that we—*you*—don't already know?" Brice asked, slightly disappointed in the big secret.

"According to my mother, it worked magically in conjunction with the family dagger, which we have."

"I know that part of the dagger is magic, and our family keeps that part a secret." Brice paused. "The stone holds magic and allows us to infuse a bit of the aether from the falls into each weapon we make for the town, right?"

His grandma nodded along with his father, who returned to his seat. "That's right, son. The aether gives us the ability to continue to reproduce weapons even almost two hundred years later. Passed down from Judson—a blacksmith—was the secret to do so. Somehow, and we don't understand it completely—maybe it would tell us in that journal, if we ever found it—the magic infusing the weapons will adapt to each race, giving them a tailored weapon for them to use with their specific talents. It's brilliant during an actual fight."

Brice smiled, imagining a weapon that could be used by a witch and then by a fae, working differently for each. "That's pretty cool. I didn't know that part."

"When you turn eighteen, that is part of your orientation into being a hunter and an official part of the businesses of the family. Brock got the background just the same so he understood everything the family went through, even though he isn't a hunter. He also helps with the weapons, which you know. He oversees and protects the underground armory at Soothing Sips since he's there every day."

"Could the journal be hidden there?" Brice thoughtfully asked.

His father shook his head. "No, because that was built after Marie and Judson's time. We've also looked in the secret area in the basement of the house as well. But so far, no luck."

Brice's excitement rose with the idea of a hunt. He found himself wanting to look for the journal. He wasn't sure whether it would be helpful, but the idea of finding it for his family was appealing. An idea suddenly came to him. He remembered what the voice had told him to ask about the dagger and now found himself quite curious. His mom hadn't participated in much of the conversation, he thought because she didn't think he should be a part of it. Not for the first time, he wondered if his mom was ashamed of him because he was different and disrupted the so-far pristine record of all female witch hunters in the family.

"Mom? What do you think of the dagger? Have you ever got to use it, like in a battle?"

Lilith, who had been quiet and appeared to be lost in thought looking at the mountains, swung her head in Brice's direction. The haunted look in her eyes pierced his soul. All the color drained out of her, and she stood abruptly to her feet, throwing her wine glass to the ground, the glass shattering.

"I told you he wasn't ready," Lilith fumed, looking to her mother and then to Reggie.

"Lilith," Reggie said, his tone low and steady.

In the past, something would trigger Brice's mom, and she would become so disconnected from the family, she would stay in her room, sometimes for days at a time. No one—at least none of the kids— knew why. Even now, Brice couldn't figure out what he said that could have triggered such an outburst.

"I blame Sunny."

"This has nothing to do with Sunny," Brice said, heat flooding his words.

His mother's eyes widened at his tone. "She shows up, and all hell suddenly breaks loose. You're going to sit there and tell me she has nothing to do with this?"

"She doesn't! She wasn't the one who told me to ask about it," Brice said, then instantly regretted it. He could feel the surge of energy shoot through his body, but just before it hit his hands he breathed in, trying to stop it. He couldn't lose control here. He just couldn't. Not yet. And he couldn't reveal he had a voice in his head—at least not until he knew who it was or why it was happening.

Lilith and Eva both swung their heads back to Brice in confusion.

"Brice, who told you to ask about it?" Eva asked.

Brice stared at Lilith, his eyes hard and set. He wasn't going to answer if she didn't have to. He folded his arms across his chest in protest.

"Who told you?" Lilith asked barely above a whisper, her teeth clenched together.

"No one."

"Sunny brings trouble. She needs to leave."

"Keep Sunny out of it, Mom." They had a momentary stare-down. Brice turned away first and inhaled sharply through his nose. "Why is it so hard to answer the question about the dagger?" Brice asked. Lilith's eyes flashed.

"Brice," his father's single word held a warning.

"No, this is ridiculous, Dad. It's a simple question."

Lilith simply turned and left, leaving everyone staring after her.

"Some things are as far from simple as they can get, son," Reggie said as he stood. He tipped his glass back and downed his beer, then gently placed the pilsner now empty of Brock's latest brew on the table. "I'll go after her."

"Sorry, Dad. Brock and I will finish any cleaning up," Brice said reluctantly.

His father nodded, then paused. "There are things you will learn soon enough, I'm afraid, then much of this will make sense."

Brice sighed and slumped back in his chair. He snuck a look at his grandma, who still sat in her seat, her back straight and her head held high, sipping on the last of her wine as she gazed up at the mountain.

"Doesn't her behavior bother you, Grandma?"

Eva turned her head to the side, offering Brice a rare sympathetic smile. "Yes, but I also understand it."

She gracefully rose from her seat and patted him on his head as she walked by.

"I wish I understood."

CHAPTER 13

"You want a ride home, little brother?" Brock asked as they closed up the winery after cleaning the mess from dinner.

"Nah. Thanks, though. Plus it's out of your way."

"Not like it's that far." Brock chuckled as they walked to the parking lot.

"True." Brice paused. "What time is it?"

"Almost eight, why?"

"Actually, if you don't mind dropping me at school, I think I might check in on the Awakening Lab tonight. Ronya said I could go. Maybe something might be helpful to me as I'm approaching such a delicate stage in my development," Brice said sarcastically.

"Nice. Well, it couldn't hurt. Even if it's about other types of awakenings and supernatural gifts, you'll need all the help you can get." Brock shrugged, then punched Brice in the arm. They both laughed and got in the truck. Brice knew his brother didn't really get it, but Brock also wouldn't look down on him for it.

"Thanks, man."

After arriving at the Academy, Brock dropped Brice off right in front. At night, the Gothic mansion took on a spookier vibe than it did during the day. Old original light fixtures glowed with an otherworldly light, ushering him into the interior courtyard. As other students walked to the evening class, their shadows played games with his mind as they grew and shrunk, depending on the way the lights flickered. He saw Ava Tate—who honestly scared him a bit after rumors of her run-in with police—as she headed in alone. He quickly made his way back to the Castor Center, where Ronya Augustine had told him to go earlier that day. He could hear her calling for everyone to take their seats just as he snuck in through the door. She spotted him and gave him a quick nod, and he found a place to sit near the back.

"Welcome, everyone, to tonight's Awakening Lab," Ronya announced as she opened the class. "If everyone one is here, let's begin."

For the next hour, Ronya used physical examples she had brought with her and even demonstrated some simple magic for the new witches in the room. Brice could feel the magic simmer beneath the skin of his forearms as she did so, but the sensation was still pretty mild in his opinion. His wrist ached, and he tried to flex it without moving it too much. Most of Ronya's teaching was geared toward the new witch or anyone dealing with magic. But she had several general topics and ideals and rules for the newly awakened supernaturals coming into their powers. He was impressed with Ronya's ability to teach and share with many different types of supes and still have it be relevant to them all. After class, he tried to duck out first, but she caught him at the door.

"Brice, I'm so glad you came tonight. Do you feel like you learned something you can help your friend with?" Ronya's eyes were bright with understanding, but also lit with a backdrop of concern. She was worried about him. He was touched.

Brice nodded. "I do. Thank you, Mrs. Augustine. It was most enlightening."

She smiled. "Good. Please come back next week if you want to."

He waved and said goodbye to her and others he saw, then quickly moved back toward the entrance of the school. As much as he didn't want to face his mom, it was time for him to go home. Not having a ride, he walked to the back of the school to find a shortcut rather than go back out front to the road. The way home through the forest and trails near the falls was a darker way to go, but it would be shorter for him to get home. He wasn't scared, but there had been plenty of stories about things happening in the forests at dark around Havenwood Falls.

"Don't think about that, Brice. Keep your mind focused and stay alert," he coached himself audibly as he walked, soon leaving the lights of the school behind.

However, he didn't get far before he stumbled upon a group of guys he knew from school—both the Academy and Havenwood Falls High. Unfortunately, they weren't friendly guys. And according to the tingles now shooting up his arms, he recognized some of them as witches. In fact, he was pretty sure one or two of them were from Chadwick Linton's group who made catcalls at Sunny in the lunchroom. Chadwick a.k.a. "Chad" was an entitled, rich jock who happened to be a witch. He was also at the skate park the day his troubles began.

"Great," he mumbled to himself. If he stopped, they would know he didn't want to face them or worse, they might think he was scared of them. He wasn't scared, but he didn't want to deal with them either. Instead, he widened his path and pretended not to see them. Maybe if he was quiet, they wouldn't . . .

"Well look who's here, boys. It's Brice Blackstone," one of them called out.

"Where's your new girlfriend, Brice?" another yelled with kissy sounds, which the others joined in chorus.

Brice kept walking, kept ignoring, kept clenching his fists so he wouldn't react.

"She's probably locked up in the loony bin for the night," another jeered while others laughed. "Maybe they only let her out during the day for good behavior."

Keep control. Don't listen to them. Brice ran mantras in his head and kept walking.

"Brice, I know you can hear me. I sense you're alarmed. Are you all right?" The voice was back.

"How do you know?"

"It doesn't matter. What's wrong?"

"Nothing I can't handle. Just bullies saying dumb stuff about a friend of mine." Brice spoke under his breath so the group wouldn't hear him and accuse him of anything.

"Does she treat you right, Brice?" one of the guys taunted with rude gestures, and the others laughed.

Brice stopped. He couldn't make his feet go any farther. Even as he tried to talk himself down, he felt the energy surging within him, building up enough to break through the dam.

"Brice, the only way to take care of bullies is to stand up to them. Don't let them make a fool of you," the voice pushed through the fog in his mind.

"I'm afraid I won't be able to control it. My hunter abilities are just now surfacing. They're witches."

"Forget trying to control it. Let it out. If they deserve it, then let them have it. It's the only way to stop them."

"What's the matter, Brice?" another from the group yelled, but then stopped and spoke to his buddies. "Hey, Chad! Maybe the problem is she won't treat him right. Is that the problem, Brice—she won't put out? She looks like she might be a tease . . . or a tramp!" They laughed.

"She's a tramp, and she won't put out to poor Brice because his power is lame!" another taunted.

Brice roared and took steps in their direction. "She is NOT a tramp. Sunny is the purest and most amazing girl, and you'll never meet anyone like her," he shouted.

"Sunny? Sunny is there?" The voice took on a new tone Brice couldn't decipher in the haze of his fury, nor did he care to.

"Oh, so she's a prude. I bet I could get her to give it up to me," the leader of the group said with a dark sneer. He tossed around a ball of light between his hands, the gesture oddly threatening.

"NO!" the voice in his head shouted at the same time Brice yelled and surged forward, releasing whatever was within him he had held back.

"Wait! Not yet," the voice spoke with an authoritative calm, enough to interrupt his blind rage.

He shot his arms out, and a bolt of light was thrown from one of his hands. The group cried out as they jumped to the sides, split down the middle.

"Whoa! Did you see that? Did he do magic?" different voices said with shock.

The leader stood tall, glaring at Brice. "Nice trick, hunter. A witch give you some fire powder?"

Brice looked down at his hands with both surprise and disgust. How could he have done that? He intended to hurt that boy but at the last second pulled back. He was so angry, but the voice stopped him. Grateful, confused, and flat-out in trouble, Brice turned and ran all the way home.

He didn't stop when he heard the group laughing at him again.

He didn't stop when he ran through a freaky part of the forest.

He didn't stop when he heard the small voice of a tree nymph utter a cry as he broke a tree branch that got in his way.

He didn't stop until he landed in his bedroom, heaving for breath while at the same time wishing for death.

CHAPTER 14

*B*rice slept fitfully that night. His dreams were a mix of him destroying Chad with magic or conversely stealing his magic, leaving him with nothing left. He tossed and turned until the early morning light pierced through his blinds and woke him up at an ungodly hour. However, because of the night he had, Brice was more than ready to wake up. He lay there, dreading going to school after what happened the night before. Finally, his alarm went off, and he got ready for school, putting on his uniform of corduroy pants, dress shirt and tie, and blue blazer. He missed being able to wear skinny black jeans, Vans, T-shirts, and hats with various skater brands on them.

Brice trudged downstairs to the kitchen for breakfast, but as soon as he heard his mom in the kitchen, he veered toward the office in hopes of escaping an encounter with her. But it was too late. She had heard him.

"Brice? Is that you? Come in here, please," she called from behind the wall.

Brice's heart fell to the floor. He had such mixed emotions regarding his mom. He didn't know what mood she would be in.

"Coming," he called anyway as he grabbed his backpack off the floor and brought it with him.

He paused in the entry to the great room and took a deep breath as he moved toward the bar-height counter where his mom read the *Sun & Moon Tribune* while drinking her coffee. She looked up, and their eyes locked on each other, neither one choosing to be the first to speak. He figured she was the parent, so he shouldn't have to.

"Brice . . ." She cleared her throat and tried again, apparently choosing a different tactic. "Your father tells me you confided in him you were experiencing some more sensations of a hunter. Is this correct?"

Brice relaxed his shoulders in relief. Even though they definitely needed to clear the air, he wasn't ready to yet. "A little bit. Maybe. I've been sensing when a witch is near and also a witch hunter."

"Do you feel me right now?" she asked, studying him as he spoke.

He paused and reflected inwardly, gauging his senses, then bit his lip. "Hmm, I guess not. Maybe it's coming and going?"

She nodded as if she figured that was the case. "It is beginning, but it seems you might have a little ways to go yet. You're not quite ready yet. However, I'd like to get your orientation started officially so we can go over any questions you might have. I know Macy made us tell you things earlier on, but I believe there might be more to discuss. Could we make an appointment for next week?" she said, opening her calendar app on her phone.

Brice frowned. "Couldn't we just talk about it at home whenever something comes up?"

Lilith frowned in return. "Don't be difficult, Brice. This is the way it's always been in our family, and it's one of our traditions. We will abide by them so we don't lose them or get off track."

Brice sighed but gave in for now. "Okay, I'll look at my school schedule. I know I have art club with Mr. Weaver at Havenwood Falls High on Tuesday after school and I'd like to go to Awakening Lab again on Thursday night. Other than my work schedule, which you know, that's all I have."

"I'll look and offer a couple options for you. I'll need to double check with the other hunters as well. They all join in on the first part of orientation." She raised her eyes over the rim of her coffee cup just before she took a sip, but he knew she was waiting for a reaction. Macy would have given her one, but Brice remained steady and simply nodded—though inside he was groaning at the rigidity of it all.

He didn't know any other supe in town who had such a rigid awakening as the witch hunters did. He supposed it stemmed from always having to prove themselves to the townspeople they weren't there to hunt the witches. He'd thought after so much time had passed they would be able to relax about it, but apparently not yet. He mentally sighed. Someday. Maybe when Dante and his rogues were gone or out of the picture for good and they didn't have to worry about them. Even with Dante in the Infernum, there seemed to be a feeling of unfinished business, like he was hanging over their shoulders. As far as Brice was aware, it was near impossible to get out of the Infernum once one was held within it; however it had happened a time or two where someone escaped the supernatural part of Hell. Brice had no idea how someone like Dante without any magic could get out, so that gave him peace.

"I'm glad you were able to use the witch's salve on your wrist. Is it healed already enough you don't need a brace?" Lilith asked, eyeing Brice's wrist with a bit of surprise.

Brice rotated his wrist more slowly than he actually could and flexed his finger. "Oh yeah, it's healing up nice."

Brice smiled, grabbed his bag and his board, and headed out the front door.

He skateboarded quite a ways down Blackstone Road before he heard a car pull up behind him. He waved the driver to go around him without looking back to see who it was. After a minute of the car creeping behind him, he turned around with frustration.

Hollis was driving Ryne's truck with Sunny sticking her head and arms out the passenger window, waving. He laughed and smiled at them as he jumped off his board. Hollis pulled up alongside him.

"Morning!" Brice said as he smiled at Sunny.

"Want a ride?" she asked with too much cheer for the early morning. He nodded, and Sunny scooted over to the middle to give him room.

When Brice got settled, he noted the tingles at the base of his neck, recognizing Sunny and Hollis as fellow hunters. The sensations had returned and felt stronger than they had the last time he saw them the night before at the vineyard. He wondered if it was because they were confined in the cab of the truck—or perhaps that had nothing to do with it.

Hollis drove down the long drive to the Academy and circled in front of the building. Both Brice and Sunny got out of the truck.

"Thanks for the ride, Hollis," Brice said with a wave, heading toward the arched entry.

"Wow, Brice, look at all the Halloween decorations!" Sunny said with great admiration as she took in the scene before them. Overnight Halloween had made an additional pass over the school and barfed décor all over. After a few more steps, both Brice and Sunny paused and slowed their movements. She looked at him with a raised eyebrow.

"Do you sense them?"

Brice nodded. "I do. The feelings have been getting stronger. They're nearby."

"Good. There are several together. So we will go around them," she said with a smile, but it seemed she had lost some of the extra enthusiasm she normally carried. Brice gave her an odd look and wondered if she *knew* something. Still learning, he would take his cues from her. They stepped to the other side of the courtyard and carried on as if nothing was out of the ordinary. "It's about trusting your instincts and listening to your heart," she added as she reached down and held Brice's hand.

He almost froze but didn't. He almost passed out from holding his breath, but thankfully he didn't. He kept his cool until the group of witches from last night—Chad's gang, as he thought of them—fanned out from their huddle in the corner and blocked the path, crossing their arms and opening their stance. There was a no-fighting policy at the Academy, and Brice didn't want to get kicked out. He would remain calm and talk his way through the group of six guys.

"Good morning, gentlemen," Sunny said with a smile.

Chadwick leered at Sunny, his eyes roving from top to bottom. Brice stepped in front of her, pulling her behind him.

"Stay away from her," Brice warned in a calm tone.

"What are you going to do about if I don't want to?" he came back. Brice remained quiet. "That's what I thought." Chadwick scoffed with a sarcastic laugh.

"We need to get to class," Brice said loud enough the other students passing by could hear. Many stopped to see what was going on. "This isn't the time or place, Chad." He gripped Sunny's hand and tried to get by the outside of the group.

"I think it's the perfect place to shut your dumb skater face up," Chadwick said.

CHAPTER 15

Several things happened at once. One of the goons reached for Sunny's arm. She squealed. A surge of energy shot through Brice like second nature. He pushed Sunny toward the wall and flung a magical energy shield in front of her to protect her, then threw a punch in the face of the guy who'd tried to pull her. Another guy—he couldn't tell which one—jumped on his back and put him in a chokehold. Brice grappled for a grip, sucking in air so he didn't pass out. Adrenaline soared through Brice, and he held the guy's wrist, then violently bent himself forward, throwing the guy over his head to land on his back. Chad came at Brice and punched him in the eye, then whispered words under his breath. A spell. He enacted a spell against Brice while he was down, clutching his eye.

Hell no. Brice shot out a hand and slammed Chad in the gut with a burst of energy that pushed him against the stone wall. He followed up by putting his other hand right in front of Chad's neck. He didn't physically touch him, but he felt the magic go to the guy's throat. He didn't squeeze. He just kept his pressure there as a threat. He didn't want to hurt the guy, no matter how angry he was at him.

"You need to leave us alone, Chad," Brice said through gritted teeth, barely holding on to control. Something else inside him felt like it was fighting, clawing its way out of his chest. His head turned fuzzy.

He tried to focus on the face in front of him. Brice was so tired of being picked on, left out, and thought less of. "I deserve respect," he added.

"Yes, Brice. Yes, you do." The voice was back, whispering in Brice's head.

Nice timing, Brice mentally shot back.

The kid was stupid enough to laugh through the magical pressure Brice put on his throat. Blood trickled out of his nose from a punch.

"You deserve nothing," Chad spat in Brice's face with a sneer.

"Borrow the witch's magic. That'll make him respect you."

How? What's happening to me? Brice asked, feeling his new and limited powers fading as he grew weaker.

"Your hunter is awakening in the presence of a witch. It's the greatest feeling, isn't it? Soak in the power, Brice."

I can't hold him much longer. He's stronger than I am.

"Your mother won't tell you this, but you can have access to your full power right now. All you have to do is pull the boy's energy out and absorb it into yourself. Your hunter will lock on. You just have to let it."

Won't that kill him? Brice asked with a rush. He could feel his metaphysical grip on Chad's neck slipping. Then he'd really be the laughingstock of the school. He'd never live that down, and Chad would never leave them alone. He'd have to homeschool or leave Havenwood Falls.

"He should be fine. Might hurt a bit, but you'll have the upper hand. He'll never bother you again. And everyone watching will respect and revere Brice Blackstone!" the male voice shouted and reveled gleefully in Brice's mind.

A crowd had gathered. Several tried to intervene and stop the fight, but the other witches from the group put up a force field that kept everyone else out. All they could do was watch. Sunny stood outside the barrier now with Hollis, who must have heard the altercation before she left the school. Brice could focus on the bully in front of him, knowing Sunny was safe.

Brice closed his eyes and let his hunter rise to the surface and take over. Within an instant, and almost too easily, he felt the magical energy siphon away from Chad. Brice didn't feel like he had control of himself; his body was on autopilot. He didn't know that would happen. The boy screamed in agony. Brice couldn't stop. He had to keep going.

He needed the energy. He needed the magic. He needed the power!

"Brice, stop!" He heard Hollis shout, but she sounded so far away. "Don't listen to him!"

Brice paused. He wasn't sure he heard Hollis right. Listen to who?

Chad struggled under his invisible hand. Brice had to focus on pulling the energy out and absorbing it into himself. The guy gasped for breath and clawed at anything he could try to grab ahold of, but Brice was just out of his reach.

"You don't want to kill him, Brice." Sunny. Her voice—her simple, non-judging voice—penetrated the fog of his mind. He gasped as he let go of the power his hunter used to suck the magic out of Chad's soul, and he flew back as the magic in his system seemed to backdraft when he completely let go of all control.

"Magic? You wielded magic?" the voice asked with complete and utter disgust. *"How could this be?"*

Brice was too exhausted to reply. Chad fell to the ground with a thud and lay limp. His goons released the shield around them and ran to his aid. Brice let Hollis pull him back and away from everyone.

"Is he . . . Did I . . . ," Brice stuttered. He tried to get up and make his way back to Chad. "I need to see . . ."

"He's all right, Brice. You didn't pull his magic out far enough. He'll be fine after a while," Hollis explained with more sensitivity than he had heard used before. Brice nodded and let her pull him back against the wall. She whispered near his ear, "This isn't good, Brice. The faculty is here. We can't make this go away."

"Everyone get to class now," Mr. Hale demanded without raising his voice. A supernatural mist rose throughout the courtyard, obscuring everyone's sight lines to Brice and Chad. He had a presence about him; people were intimidated by him and students feared him.

"Members of the Court of the Sun and the Moon are on their

way." His gaze—though his eyes couldn't be seen well behind his ever-present sunglasses—bored into Chad. "Chadwick Linton, your parents are also on their way," he said, though Chad lay on the ground, still unconscious. He then swiveled his head toward Brice. "Brice Blackstone, you will accompany the members of the Court into town, where your parents will find you."

Brice nodded. He knew better than to say anything at this point. Mr. Damien Hale hadn't been in Havenwood Falls too long. He had transferred under mysterious circumstances from another school where he taught. Brice didn't know much about him other than he was a hellhound and he was a single guy who kept to himself. Mr. Hale turned and went back into the school, fully expecting his orders to be followed.

Brice leaned his head back against the cool gray stone and sighed. He was in so much trouble, but more than that, he had no idea what it was he had even done to Chad. He opened one eye and could see the rise and fall of Chad's chest. One of his buddies stayed with him as well as the secretary, who must have been told to watch them until those responsible for each of them had come.

"It will be okay, Brice. You'll see," Sunny said, then added, "Remember we're on your side."

"I'll try," Brice croaked out when he saw a shiny black sedan pull up right in front of the school. Saundra Beaumont, Michaela Petran, and Addie Beaumont got out of the car. Another vehicle pulled up behind them, and Sheriff Kasun got out.

"The sheriff is here, too?" Brice groaned.

The group walked over to where they were. Saundra knelt down in front of Chad and felt his head, then his chest. She rose to her feet and faced Brice with a grim expression.

"Brice Blackstone, did you do this?" Saundra gestured down at Chad.

Brice slowly stood. "I did."

The buzzing sensations in his arms became more agitated with their added presence. Saundra was not only in a high position within the Court, but she was also one of the leaders of the Luna Coven and a very powerful witch at that.

"How? Chadwick was attacked with magic, and it seems his magical energy is stressed," Addie provided her own assessment.

"Looks like history finally came back around," Saundra said under her breath.

Brice gave her an odd look, trying to understand what she meant, when he realized she knew Marie and Judson. Saundra would have been young, but she would remember them. He couldn't believe he didn't think to talk to her or others who were still around from that time period.

"Well, let's get this over with." She held out her hand, palm up, in front of Brice.

"What do you propose we do?" Michaela asked. She looked from Addie, one of her best friends, to Saundra.

"Brice, please hold out your hands," Saundra instructed.

Brice did so and watched as she said a spell and a magical cuff encircled his wrists, binding them together. His eyes widened, and he hoped none of the kids from his class could see him. He glanced over to Sunny, but she seemed unfazed by what was happening and gave him an encouraging nod accompanied by a quick smile.

"Handcuffs, Grandma? Is that really necessary? He's not going anywhere," Addie questioned. She pushed her sunglasses to the top of her nose and put her hands on her waist. Addie was a witch and in the last year had found out she was also part hellhound. Brice noted she caught Mr. Hale's attention through the window and gave him a curt nod.

"It is standard procedure, Adelaide," she said.

"It's okay," Brice quietly said. He deserved it. He hurt someone, and so he deserved to be handcuffed. He watched Saundra do something interesting with her hands and then whisper some words before she placed her hands on Chad's chest.

"Brice Blackstone, you are under arrest for the attack on Chadwick Linton. You will come with me, and your parents will meet you at the prison, as you are still underage," Sheriff Kasun explained.

Brice gave Sunny and Hollis one last look of defeat, then he simply went to the truck and waited for the sheriff to let him in. He spared a quick glance at Chad, relieved to see him coming to and being helped to sit up by Saundra.

Brice got shut into the cab of the truck. "Take me to jail, Sheriff."

CHAPTER 16

*B*rice sat on the hard bench up against a cool stone wall in his prison cell. He never thought he would see the inside of a cell in his lifetime, especially not while still underage. Sheriff Kasun had told him he was just being held until his parents came to collect him. He also mentioned that the Court would be involved but he didn't know to what extent—if he would have to have a trial or not. The police station was to the east of City Hall and was small, with only two cells for humans and other special cells for supernaturals.

Leaning his head against the stone, he had time to think. It all had happened so fast, Brice wasn't even sure exactly all that did happen. How had he used magic? Did he really use magic or was it a fluke with his hunter awakening? He could try to explain it away as much as he wanted, but deep down Brice knew he accessed magic. He just couldn't comprehend how. The voice that had been in the back of his mind the last several days was mysteriously quiet. During his encounter with Chad, it felt like the voice was right there with him, even enforcing its will through Brice. He was pretty sure he wasn't possessed. Wouldn't someone know if they were? And if he claimed "the voice made him do it," he was pretty sure that wouldn't go over well with anyone—except maybe Sunny, since she had her own voices.

Brice thought of Sunny and hoped she was all right. He tried to protect her the best he could in that moment, but he didn't have much time to check on her and see. It was strange, now he had time to think on it, how the voice seemed to know Sunny. And Hollis had made reference to not "listening to him," when Brice hadn't told her—or Sunny, for that matter—anything about his voice. Irritation crept up through his chest. How could the voice just leave him hanging like that?

"Hey! Are you there?" Brice said out loud, forgetting where he was.

"I'm here, Brice. What do you need?" Sheriff Kasun responded from down the hall.

Brice backpedaled, unsure what to say. "Uh . . . do you know how much longer my parents are going to be?" That should work.

"Your dad just called and said they would be here in ten minutes. Hang in there, son. You won't have to stay too much longer."

"Thanks, Sheriff."

Brice tried again, but this time he closed his eyes and thought of the voice. He thought of the cadence in the way he spoke, and the timbre of his tone. He directed his energy toward wherever that voice had come to him from. Without truly understanding it, Brice accessed the energy he had felt move through him before, and then it suddenly stopped, as if hitting a brick wall. Brice wasn't sure what to do now, so he guessed.

Hello? Are you there?

"*Brice? How did you contact me?*" the voice said with a hint of alarmed surprise, or even a hint of anger—Brice couldn't tell for certain through the connection.

I backtracked the way it feels when you speak to me. Brice mentally shrugged like it wasn't that hard to figure out. *What happened earlier? What did you have me do?* Brice felt himself getting worked up and slowly inhaled, calming his racing heart.

"*I simply helped you access the power you have within you as a witch hunter. You shouldn't have to suppress it and be treated like a caged animal until their appointed time. You and I are destined to work together, to be an unstoppable team. Be free and be who you are meant to be! I helped you become powerful!*"

Brice had a moment of confusion, torn between liking the feeling of being powerful and afraid of what it could do to him. The uncertainty of the voice's identity weighed on him. Though he was afraid to admit it, he had an idea of who the speaker was.

"Is he speaking to you, Brice?" a woman's voice interrupted his connection.

Brice startled and opened his eyes to find Hollis standing on the other side of the bars, watching him intently.

"What are you talking about?" Brice played dumb and looked away from her eyes.

"My father. He recently tried to talk to me, but because of the new wards around me, he had a hard time getting through. But because you're in a transition period with fluctuating energy, the wards aren't quite as strong until you turn eighteen and reinforce your commitment to the town," Hollis explained, as if she were an old veteran of Havenwood Falls protocol.

"Your father?" Brice stood. The color drained from his face, and he felt light-headed. He didn't want to acknowledge it, but hearing her say it out loud confirmed his own suspicions.

Hollis watched him and nodded knowingly.

"How could he even do that? He's in the Infernum, and he doesn't have that ability, does he?"

Hollis shrugged. "There are ways. Maybe he has a witch working for him even in there. I chose to ignore him, and he went away, frustrated to not get through to me."

"Anyway, he's not speaking to me. I don't know what you mean."

Hollis gave him a small smile and shrugged her shoulders. "Well, that's good then. I just wanted to make sure and get a moment with you before your mom gets here."

Brice sat back down. "Thanks, Hollis. I appreciate you checking on me."

Hollis turned and left down the hall, leaving him to his thoughts once more. Her father? No, he didn't think that was possible.

Are you still there? Brice went back into his mind. He needed to find out for himself.

"I'm here. I'll always be here for you. Seems I might be the only one that gets you. You need the power, unlike the others, don't you? You can handle it better than they could. That's why they make everyone wait for it, because they can't handle it. But you can."

Brice rubbed his eyes then pinched his nose. Some of the words hit him as truth. He once more felt confused by all the rules they had to abide by in Havenwood Falls. If everyone would simply trust him with information and include him without all the secrecy, they wouldn't be in this mess. This was their fault. He knew deep down that wasn't true, but he was angry, alone, and wanted someone to blame.

You're right.

"Of course I am. Now, what is this nonsense of you using magic? You don't need filthy magic unless it advances your needs. You and I are the same in that way."

I . . . I don't know exactly. I think I have magic, my own magic.

"Impossible!" the voice roared.

Well, is it? If a witch and a witch hunter had children, isn't it possible one might have magic? Brice asked, suddenly thinking of Marie and Judson. But as far as anyone knew, Judson didn't have magic.

"That is an abomination! Our kind does not mix with their *kind. That's what your sister couldn't seem to let go of. That is her failure."*

Brice scrunched his face. The pieces to his puzzle were beginning to create a pretty strong case regarding who he spoke with. And he didn't like his sister being involved in whatever this was. He started to feel wary of the voice. His strong feelings about mixing of the types of supernaturals was a bit harsh considering he didn't know any of them personally—again adding to the clues stacking up.

"I know more than you might think, being where I am."

Where are you? Brice asked suspiciously.

"In a cage, similar to yours. Time to go. Stay away from the magic, Brice, or I won't help you."

What? How can you say that? What if I need help? Hello? Brice asked over and over, but there was a mental block. How did he do that?

"Brice?" his father's voice penetrated his mental preoccupation.

"Dad!" He rushed up to the bars. "Is Mom here too?"

Reggie nodded. "She's talking to the sheriff, then will be right here. Go easy on her, Brice. This is harder on her than she's letting on."

"Hard on *her*?" Brice said with an outraged whisper. "What about me? I don't know what the hell is going on with me!"

"That's what I want to know," Lilith sternly said as she walked into the cell area.

"Mom," Brice acknowledged, but sat back down.

"I thought you might like to know Chadwick Linton will recover just fine. The Court has agreed to not arraign you based on your age, but is requiring that you undergo not only your orientation into being a witch hunter, but also community service."

"Community service?" Brice complained. "He started it."

"And you could have killed him!" his mom shot back. "Be grateful his parents aren't pressing charges. It was all Saundra and I could do to keep them from coming down here themselves. And I wouldn't blame them. What the hell happened out there, Brice? How could you lose control like that?" Lilith's voice rose and something akin to shock filled her expression. Her voice lowered and tightened as if the words choked her throat, and she gripped the bars. "How could you not know what you were doing to that boy? How could you do this to me again?"

She gasped and folded in on herself. Brice watched something transpire in his mom he hoped he would never see. She was broken. Her control slipped, and she instantly seemed a shell of the woman she normally was.

"Mom?" Brice asked, then looked to his dad, who placed his hand on her lower back with tears in his eyes.

"Brice, this is my fault. This is all my fault." She appeared to be having a revelation. So as long as she wasn't blaming him, Brice remained quiet and let her continue.

Lilith turned haunted eyes on her husband who, with understanding, nodded encouragement to her. "Go ahead, Lilith. It's time you let this go. To help your son, you need to deal."

"Eighteen years ago, I killed a boy . . . a witch."

"What?" Brice practically shouted. How did they not know about that?

80

"I was having a hard time conforming to all my mother's rules and the traditions of the town. I wasn't sure if their way was how I truly wanted to live. Even though I already had your brother and sister, I felt I was missing out on something. I left town and found Dante and his rogue witch hunters. I lived with them for a season. I trained with them and worked with them and one day, I killed with them. I had a reality check when I realized I was pregnant with you, and I knew I didn't want to live like those Blackstones lived. I missed my family and determined that from that day on, we would live by the traditions and rules of our town and our Blackstone hunters even more than before. Not long after I had you, I took Aunt Letti's seat on the Court. Then when Macy ran away a couple years ago and found Dante, I realized my actions had more of an effect on my children than I thought. In my efforts to protect you all and myself, I ended up pushing you all away. And I . . . I'm sorry, Brice."

Brice's mouth hung wide open. He looked back and forth between his father and his mother. A bomb had dropped, and he didn't know what to do . . . what to say.

"I . . . uh . . .wow, what to say after that . . . Thank you for being honest, Mom. Wow. We always knew you carried around something big, but we had no idea what it could be."

Brice sat back down and stared at his parents through the bars. "Now what?"

CHAPTER 17

*S*heriff Kasun entered right at that moment and unlocked Brice's cell. "You can use the conference room if you would like some privacy, or you can stay here. Whatever suits your needs."

"Thanks, Ric. I think we'll just take a few more minutes and sit here with Brice," Reggie said. They entered the cell and sat on either side of him on the bench.

"Now, Brice, tell us what happened, please," Lilith said with a softer tone.

"Chad and his goons—who happen to be witches—had been giving me a hard time at school. Since Sunny arrived, they added her into the mix. We tried to enter the school, and they blocked us. One of them tried to pull Sunny, and I lost it. I hit him."

"Like physically?" his dad asked.

Brice nodded. "I punched him in the nose."

"He deserved that," Lilith said, to both their surprise. "What? They manhandled a girl against her will. Continue."

"Then the fighting started. I somehow threw out a magical shield and pushed Sunny out of the way. One got on my back, and I threw him over my shoulders, then Chad was working up a spell. He was going to use magic against me. I defended myself, and instinctively, I threw out a lightning bolt type energy that pushed him against the wall. It held him there. He said nasty things. I got closer to him. I was so angry." He paused, reliving the moment and taking a breath. "Then I felt my hunter side take over, and I pulled at his magical energy." He stopped and looked at his parents. They hadn't said anything. "That's it. That's what happened."

"First, you defended yourself and your friend. I would expect nothing less," his dad interjected, and his mom agreed.

"Secondly, I didn't pay attention to the signs, or give you the opportunity to share with me that you were having symptoms of your hunter reawakening," his mom added. So far Brice was liking the direction this talk was headed. "But Brice, we don't understand how you think you used magic. Witch hunters don't have active magic. You know this."

"Could one of the witches be playing a prank on you? Or would one of your friends make it look like you did magic?" his dad asked.

Instantly deflated, Brice lost hope in their conversation. "No. No one would do that. I did magic. And I have nothing further to say if you don't believe that." He moved his wrist back and forth. "How do you explain my wrist all healed?"

"I gave you the witch's salve, Brice. Although, that does seem awfully fast even for that assistance." His mom examined his wrist and cocked her head with a frown.

"Why don't we take this home and continue to talk about it? Brice, we're not saying we don't believe you. We just don't understand yet," his dad tried to explain as they all got up and walked out of the cell.

With goodbyes to Sheriff Kasun and release papers signed, they left to head home. Brice felt lost again. He thought something amazing had just happened with his parents, and it had, but it only lasted but a moment. Once again, he didn't know why he was the outcast in his family. He stared out the window of the backseat of the car, watching the town pass by in a blur. His mind fogged over, and he heard the voice loud and clearer than it had been before.

"Brice. I was harsh before. I didn't think it possible for you to wield magic, but I believe you. I still believe we are destined to be a team."

Can you help me understand how to use my hunter? I think the magic is fighting with it inside me. But it feels strong and wants to be dominant.

"*I will help you. I know a witch in town who will help you, too, if you tell her I sent you.*"

Brice thought over the proposition for a second. This was it. Final confirmation. *I need to know who you are.*

"*First, I'll tell you your friend Sunny had a vision long ago where we of the same name were together. Then I disappeared, and you took my place. It meant you are to be my successor, and I am to be your mentor.*"

Brice didn't like the sound of that. He also didn't like that Sunny would have had a vision about him that important and not told him about it. Perhaps he shouldn't have trusted her so fast. But that thought broke his heart.

Are you telling me your name is Brice? Brice couldn't help himself.

He heard a haughty chuckle in his mind. "*No, I'm saying there are two Dantes.*"

Silence. Hollis was right. Somehow Dante was communicating with him from the Infernum.

Shit. His forehead broke out in a cold sweat, his hands grew clammy, and his breathing escalated. He thought he might pass out. And yet he had also wanted Dante's help. Brice felt sick.

"Dad, pull over. I'm going to be sick," he said through a hand covering his mouth. Reggie pulled the car over right next to the cemetery on their way home after having to run a quick errand at Miller's Plaza. Brice threw open the door and jumped out, falling to all fours on the grass to the side of the road.

"Brice, are you okay?" his dad said, coming up next to him. His mom stood nearby, looking uncertain of her role for the first time. She had never been very maternal before. He didn't think she needed to start now.

Brice nodded. "I think so."

"*Brice, we are meant to be a team. I will help you in a way that no one else can. I have experience and connections that could all be yours if you let me pass them on to you.*"

No, this isn't the way it's supposed to be. Sunny was wrong.

"Sunny is never wrong!" the voice shouted in his mind. The fog grew to where Brice could barely think for himself. He had flashes of things in his mind's eye he didn't even know about. He saw Sunny. He saw Chad holding Sunny with a knife. He felt his feet begin to move, to run so fast he almost couldn't keep up with them.

"Brice! Brice!" He barely heard his parents' voices as they grew distant.

Sunny. Sunny was all Brice could think about. Something bad was going to happen to Sunny if he didn't get there soon.

Brice absently realized he ran through the cemetery proper for the humans. The lawns were meticulously cared for and the headstones were neatly kept. He was compelled. He couldn't stop if he wanted to. In the back of his mind he wondered if Dante was somehow controlling his movements, but the other part of him that cared for Sunny beyond anything he had ever felt before didn't care. He had to get to her.

Swiftly, he followed the path to the stone-pillared arch leading to the tunnel that went under Blackstone Road. He came out in the other side of the cemetery—the supernatural side. This section was far less neat and tidy, but he could feel the sacredness, even as fast as he ran. Vaguely, he noted he ran toward the section of mausoleums near the back. His arms crawled with the tingly sensation indicating the presence of magic; the wards in this part were extremely strong and very old.

He came to an abrupt stop in front of one of the oldest structures. The gray stone was intact, but chips and pieces of it had crumbled with time and weather. But what he couldn't stop staring at was the sight of Sunny standing before him.

And the sight of Chadwick Linton standing behind her with one arm around her neck in a head lock and the other holding a knife poised at her throat.

"Sunny."

CHAPTER 18

*B*rice quickly caught his breath. He was afraid to move. He didn't know what to do. Chad had an evil sneer across his face as he proceeded to slowly poke the tip of the knife into Sunny's perfect, smooth, porcelain neck. His eyes found hers. She was calm, and her eyes held a deep well of emotion. She smiled at him. He couldn't believe it. He guessed when someone knew what was going to happen, they could be prepared for it.

"I was waiting for you. I knew you would come," Sunny said. Brice smiled at her.

"Of course I did. I will always come for you, Sunny." And in that moment, Brice realized it was true. Sunny had found a way into his heart.

"I know." She smiled again at him.

"Shut up. Both of you!" Chad said, wiggling the knife back and forth to remind them he still held it.

"Chad, don't do this," Brice said with an even tone, not wanting to scare him into to doing something even more stupid.

"Chad's not here at the moment, Brice," the voice he had heard in his mind said out loud through Chad's mouth.

Dante.

"How are you doing this? Why are you doing this?" Brice questioned.

Chad's eyes were vacant. The only thing Brice could think of was one of his zombie video games. Chad was Dante's puppet.

"Because, Brice, I need you. I already told you we are meant to be a team. And now that you have magic, I realized it can lend to my agenda."

"Which is what?" Brice asked, feeling like he wasn't getting something important.

"With enough magic, I can escape this hellish place," he spat out.

"Is it even possible for you to escape the Infernum?" Brice asked.

"He figured out how to use a very powerful witch also in the Infernum to communicate out," Lilith explained, coming up behind Brice with his father. "Apparently, he also is using her to manipulate bodies as well." She gestured toward Chad and Sunny. Brice was sure he was also being manipulated physically both just now and earlier at the school.

At that moment, Sunny cried out in pain. Chad had pierced her skin with the knife.

"I expect you to pay attention to me," Dante said, using Chad's voice. "Hello, Lilith. It's good to see you again. I've been instructing your boy. You've been neglecting him in such a time of transition. Someone had to step in."

"Dante. I'll take it from here," she said with complete control, not giving him the fight he sought after. She stood tall and strong, fierce as she always did in a battle, but something new—confidence in herself perhaps—came through as she spoke. Brice admired his mom for maybe the first time, understanding more of what she had been through. He supposed that was part of growing up: seeing your parents' faults and realizing they were fallible and doing the best they could too, making mistakes and everything. Just like he had.

"Dante, you came for me. Let Sunny go and deal with me," Brice said. His mom gave him a look that said she wasn't happy with his tactic. He shrugged. This was his mess. He intended to see it through, whatever the outcome.

"I like this boy, Lilith. That is why you named him after me, isn't it? Because you knew we were ultimately destined to be together, for me to take him under my wing and train him as my own."

Dante was demented, but apparently he believed it.

Lilith was about to say something, but Brice held up his hand to stop his mother. Brice moved slowly closer toward the mausoleum.

"Let her go, Dante. You don't need her. You need me," Brice coaxed.

"You're right. I don't need her," Dante spat, then took the knife and stabbed her in the side as he shoved her away.

"No!" Brice shouted, about to run after her, but Dante quickly changed tactics and put the knife to himself—or to Chad.

Sunny stumbled into Lilith's arms. Reggie typed something into his phone, then helped lay Sunny on the ground. Sunny waved at Brice, letting him know she would be okay.

"That wasn't necessary, Dante," Brice scolded, his voice taking on a strange new authority.

"I needed assurance." The sight was strange. It looked as if Chad was about to take his own life, holding a knife to his own neck at an odd angle.

"What do you need from me?"

"Take his magic. Absorb the energy of his soul into your being as soon as I say," Dante instructed with vehemence.

Brice didn't know enough about how that part of him worked, so he agreed.

"No, Brice. You don't understand what that will do to you," his mom pleaded from behind him.

He turned his head and looked into his mom's eyes. Yeah, he had an idea what it might do to him. Then his gaze found Sunny's. The confidence she held in her eyes for him made all the difference.

Brice stepped forward, closer to Chad. Being that close when he wasn't fighting him felt awkward and anticlimactic, but he positioned himself to be within range.

"Okay, Dante. I'm ready. Let's be a team."

Chad let out a maniacal laugh. The sight would haunt Brice the rest of his life, if he lived much longer. Unexpectedly, Dante shoved Chad's own hand with the knife into his chest. A gurgled scream pierced the air.

At the same time, Brice felt a hand at his back.

"Take this," his mom whispered into his ear while he felt a sharp sting in the palm of his hand. He flinched but didn't lash out like he wanted to. Then she gripped his hand around the hilt of a sword. He was familiar with that feeling, working with the weapons in their basement. He nodded but kept it behind his back. Did his mom want him to finish Chad off?

Just as Chad's body slumped to the ground, he heard Dante's voice back in his mind. *"It's time, Brice. Do it now!"*

Brice knelt on the ground over Chad's body and placed a hand on his chest. He barely felt Chad's life force. His breathing was low and shallow.

No. This is not how this was supposed to happen. Brice leaned forward, closed his eyes, and let his hunter come to the surface. He inhaled deep and slow, imagining himself taking the energy from Chad, while hoping to keep him alive.

"The dagger, Brice. Use it," Lilith said.

He pulled what he thought was a sword from behind his back and looked at it. It was the family dagger they used with the creation of weapons. He frowned when he saw red smeared over the hilt. His blood. It covered the now glowing stone set in the middle.

Glowing. The dagger glowed!

Brice's hunter pulled at Chad's witch energy against his will. But then Brice felt the other energy within him. He felt magic surging forward in his body. The magic collided with his hunter. He could feel the tug-of-war within his chest. He struggled to focus. The dagger grew brighter and brighter. He didn't stab Chad with it but instead laid it against his chest and made his intentions clear.

His hunter pulled and pulled, then combined with the magic and with a great burst, pushed it back into Chad instead. Chad's body lit up like a star in the sky. Brice pushed the magic further and further, sending it along the mental channel he felt connected with Dante until he heard a bloodcurdling scream in his mind.

Brice blacked out.

CHAPTER 19

hen Brice came to, he was once more in his bedroom. Maybe the entire thing was a dream. He rolled over and closed his hand, but pain shot through it. He looked and saw a bandage around the center of his hand where his mom had sliced him.

Nope. Not a dream. A nightmare. Had Dante killed Chad while Brice stood by and watched? He almost didn't want to know what had happened. He got up and went to his window. The sun was making its way down for the evening. All he wanted to do was go back to bed, but he needed to face the music.

Downstairs he heard voices in the kitchen. A lot of voices.

"Brice! Hey, Brice is awake," Macy shouted as she ran and threw her arms around him, practically choking him with her hug.

"Hi, Mace, what's going on?"

"Macy, let him breathe," his mom scolded as she came over to look at him. Instead of keeping her distance, though, Lilith looked at him, then brought him in for an awkward hug.

"I'm so glad you're okay, Brice. You scared us like you'll never know," she said.

"What's going on here?" Brice asked and rubbed the sleep out of his eyes.

"We're beginning your orientation and having family dinner, too,"

Macy said. "Mom and Dad are springing for Napoli's pizza!"

Brice looked around the room and saw almost everyone: Macy went to stand with Gallad, who helped get out paper plates. Grandma Eva stood near the window and smiled at him. Aunt Letti and her husband, Uncle Tranner, the dragon shifter, were outside on the patio with his father and Brock, and as he scanned the room, he realized the only people not there were Hollis, Ryne, and Sunny. He frowned.

"They are on their way, don't worry," Aunt Letti said as she entered the house.

"Is Sunny okay, Mom? Shouldn't she be in the hospital?" Brice couldn't help but remember how Chad who was Dante had stabbed her in the side. His throat bobbed.

"She is just fine. Luckily, Sunny had told the Luna Coven and Dr. Underwood to be at the cemetery at that precise moment. They were able to heal her immediately," Lilith explained.

Brice's shoulders relaxed. "Good. That's good." He looked back to his mom. "What about . . ." He dreaded the possible answer.

"Chad?" Eva impatiently supplied for him. Brice nodded gratefully.

"Chad's going to be fine," Gallad said from the other side of the room. When Brice swiveled his head in Gallad's direction, he continued. "I checked in on him this morning at the clinic, since he's part of the coven."

Brice nodded, then paused. "Wait, this morning?"

"Brice, it's Sunday. You've been asleep for two days," Macy said, her face holding concern for him.

"I slept for two days? Whoa." Brice shoved his flopping hair out of his eyes and inhaled. "That's kinda cool!" He smiled, then laughed with so much relief that he didn't kill Chad or Sunny. He might not have been holding the knife, but it was because of him they were both involved.

"What else did I miss?" he asked.

Macy moved back in a little closer to him. "Mom told us everything she told you while you were in jail. Makes so much more sense, doesn't it?"

Brice nodded. "Yeah, crazy, right?"

"She's been acting different since you've been asleep. Like . . ." She chewed the inside of her cheek while she thought of a word to describe their mom. "Like . . . nicer!"

"I heard that, Macy Marie Blackstone," Lilith said from the kitchen.

Macy punched Brice in the shoulder. "I still can't believe my little brother was in jail."

Brice huffed. "That's the part you're focusing on?" He shook his head. "Go for it. Makes things easier for me."

"We want to know, but we're waiting for the rest of the family to get here," Macy added. Brice understood and nodded. They wanted to know the rest of the story from his perspective, but they would wait for everyone.

At that same moment, the front door opened.

"We're here. Can we come in?" Hollis shouted.

"Of course, dears, come in," Aunt Letti yelled back. And into the great room walked Ryne holding several Napoli's pizza boxes and a big smile on his face. Behind him Hollis also carried several of the same boxes.

"We have the pizza!" Sunny said with a playful shout as she skipped in behind them. She instantly spotted Brice and went straight for him. "Brice!" she said and threw her arms around his neck and hugged him tight. He wrapped his arms around her waist and hugged her back. He even added in a twirl, lifting her off the ground. She giggled, and he put her down.

"How is it you are all here when I woke up?" he asked, curious.

"Sunny," they all said in unison, to which she smiled and shrugged.

He gave Sunny a secret look and whispered, "Do they know about your gift?"

She nodded with enthusiasm. "I had to explain why I told them all to be at specific places at specific times."

It seemed the Blackstones were ready to tell all—at least to each other.

They all grabbed their pizza and went outside to sit on the patio and enjoy the last of the daylight before the sun set.

Brice took a few bites, then asked, "So what happened after I blacked out at the cemetery?"

Reggie stood from his seat. "Not much, actually. The Luna Coven arrived just as the light exploded from the dagger and had Sunny and Chad taken to the medical center. They checked you out as well, but as you had simply passed out from exhaustion and spent magic, we took you home."

"And what about . . ." Brice hesitated, especially as his gaze landed on Hollis's, then figured he'd just out with it. "What about Dante?"

Lilith pursed her lips. "I don't know how you did it, but according to the hellhounds that guard the Infernum, there was a burst of light inside the prison and a shower of ash. You . . . extinguished Dante." She also glanced quickly at Hollis. He was a bad man, but he was still her father—or had been.

"Hollis . . ." Brice started, but he really didn't know what to say.

"Don't be sorry, Brice. I've had a couple days to process it, but in truth I had to process him and all he had done and him going to the Infernum months ago. You did what you had to do to protect people and your town." Hollis offered him a small smile.

"I'm sorry I lied to you when you came to me while I was in jail. I'd been hearing your father, but I didn't know for sure it was him until then. There may have been some part of me that thought it might have been, but I didn't want to believe I would have been so naive and desperate to listen to him."

"I've been there, Brice. I get it. And I knew you were, but wanted you to come to it on your own." She gave him a nod, acknowledging that he did come to it.

"So the big question on everyone's mind is: how does Brice have magic?" Macy bluntly asked.

"I had the opportunity to speak with Saundra Beaumont while Brice was asleep," Letti began as she put her food on the table. "She was there when Marie and Judson were alive. She was young then, but she said she remembered them and what happened. She and the others who also were around during that time took an oath not to reveal their secret until it was time to be revealed."

"What does that even mean, Letti? Get on with it," Eva prodded.

"I'm getting there, Eva. Hold your horses. What she said was that sometime after Marie and Judson had arrived in Havenwood Falls, Judson discovered, with the help of the aether in the water from the falls, that he actually was a witch." There was a collective gasp. "He had been spelled to hide his magic for his protection apparently from a feuding coven, but he never knew it. The Luna Coven unbound his magic, and he became a practicing witch. Then, after their children were born with both witch hunter tendencies and magic, things went wrong. They didn't know how to guide the children, and their counterparts were at war within themselves. After some trouble, they all—including the children—decided to spell the children's magic side, allowing only the hunter side to come out. For the sake of the children and ease of the bloodline, they didn't pass down that information and locked it away with the Blackstone journal."

Everyone remained quiet for a moment.

"Wow, that's a lot," Macy said. "So why don't any of the rest of us have magic, as well?"

"Because the spell was broken when I broke my oath as a witch hunter," Lilith said with some revelation.

"Do I have to have that part suppressed, too, then?" Brice asked with disappointment.

"I don't know, Brice," Lilith answered. "Do you think you can manage both sides?"

Brice thought for a moment and honestly replied. He also thought of the future for Macy and Gallad; they would be in a similar situation to Marie and Judson's. He wanted to try for their sake as well. "I think so. I would like to try."

Lilith nodded. "I'll appeal to the Court, then. As long as you can learn to control it and we don't have any issues, I don't see why you would have to."

Brice smiled. For the first time, he felt his mom heard him and respected him as a person and as a member of their family.

CHAPTER 20

$\mathcal{B}$rice performed community service as his punishment required by the Court of the Sun and the Moon. Hollis and Sunny had just picked him up in Ryne's truck from the police station. Brice got in the car and instantly reached for Sunny. She smiled and gave her hand to him. Since things had calmed down, Brice and Sunny had gone out on several dates. She had told him they would be together, and in his mind, it was forever.

They were turning onto Blackstone Road to take them up to the Blackstone house for family Taco Night when Sunny gasped with glee and gripped Brice's hand hard.

"Sunny, what is it?" he asked, while Hollis slammed her foot on the brakes, abruptly stopping the truck.

"I know where it is!"

"Where what is?" Hollis asked, and glanced at Brice, who shrugged.

"The journal. I know where it is! Well, kind of," she said, then frowned.

Brice turned toward her in the small cab of the truck. "The Blackstone journal?" Sunny nodded profusely. "Where, Sunny?"

She closed her eyes and said, "At the vineyard. I see grapes. I see bookshelves. I see a stone room with a box."

Brice frowned. "That's a little vague, but let's head to the vineyard!"

Once there, they searched in all the outbuildings and even recruited Aunt Letti, who was working there at the time. Taking a break, they went inside the main lobby for NamaStays Inn and sat in the couches. Frustrated, Brice looked around and noted how the decor in that building was as rustic modern as the winery and the tasting bar, Soothing Sips.

"Aunt Letti, this building was here first, right? I mean, our house was not the first place Marie and Judson lived, right?"

"Correct. They lived here first while they built the vineyard and then as it succeeded, they built the bigger house—your house—sometime later. Why?" she questioned.

Brice stood and slowly moved around the room, examining it. "Well, we renovated it when we updated the other buildings for the winery. So I'm imagining what it might have been like as their home."

"Well, the rooms upstairs would have been bedrooms, similar to what they are now. The kitchen would be the same. We opened up a wall over there to create a bigger sitting area." She pointed to the area just before the hall.

Brice's eyes widened as he spotted a row of bookshelves. "Sunny! Didn't you see bookshelves? Do these look familiar?"

Sunny ran over and studied them. She smiled, then nodded. "Yep, those are them!"

"Brice, I hate to burst your bubble, but we've examined all the books in those shelves and the secret basement behind it. The Court knew all about it, as this was the original weapon cache. It was close to Judson's forge and had easy access to store them. We had the very thought that you do: that perhaps the ancestors would have left information or anything pertinent to the family, such as a journal. But over the years we found nothing."

Brice frowned. "I'm going to do my own search, if that's okay."

"Go for it."

"Brice, I didn't see the book in the shelf. I saw a box in a stone room," Sunny reminded him.

"Right. Let's just look to make sure we aren't missing something."

Brice, Sunny, and Hollis spent the next several minutes looking at all the spines and examining different books. But came up with nothing. "Hey, Aunt Letti, can you tell me how to open the bookcase?"

Aunt Letti shook her head in denial. "No way. This is your adventure. You can figure it out."

She gave him a wink and a sneaky smile.

Disappointed, Brice put his hand on one of the books—he didn't even look which one—and pulled it out. Something clicked and a mechanism whirled. Brice jumped back and watched in awe as the bookshelf moved to the side.

"Whoa!" Reggie and Hollis said simultaneously, as Reggie entered the room.

"Looks like you found it," Aunt Letti said with a smile, straightening up a pile of papers on the front desk counter.

"Call the family, please, Letti," Reggie said, watching the bookshelf move seemingly on its own as it opened up into a doorway with stairs leading down.

Reggie stuck his head into the hole next to Brice's. "What do you think, Dad?"

"Well, it's been searched multiple times, but there's nothing wrong with a fresh pair of eyes." Reggie peered down into darkness.

"We're going to need some flashlights." But just as Brice took one step down, light illuminated the stairwell. "Or it could be made with a spell that defies time itself," Brice said with awe.

"That is awesome," Hollis said, watching from behind with Sunny, her face an expression of pure joy.

"Go ahead. I'll let Lilith know where you are when she gets here," Letti said, shooing them to go explore.

Brice, Reggie, Hollis, and Sunny all made their way down the stairs into a decent-sized stone room. It didn't make up the entire footprint of the house, but it was at least the size of the living room area upstairs. Floor-to-ceiling gray stone surrounded them on all four sides. A few weapons still hung on the walls, ready and waiting to be used. A large, long metal slab upon wooden triangles for legs created a type of worktable. The room was covered in dust, and cobwebs graced every corner and edge.

"Anybody see anything resembling a journal?" Hollis doubtfully asked, running a finger down the table, leaving a trail in the dust behind her. Each of them looked around the room, but there weren't too many places anything could hide.

"I saw a box," Sunny said. "It had pretty details on it, but I don't see it here."

Reggie silently studied the room, calculating something under his breath.

"What is it, Dad?"

"Something is off about the stonework in this area." He walked over to one wall and pointed out a section with his finger, drawing the outline of a shape for the others to see. "I've never noticed it before."

"I see it!" Brice said with excitement. He ran his hands over the area. "It feels different too."

The others each took a turn, wanting to feel what had Brice and his dad in a quandary.

"This is it!" Sunny clapped her hands.

"What's it?" Hollis asked.

"The journal, it's in there," she said, with an expression saying it was obvious. "It's Brice's turn!"

Reggie looked at Brice with a question in his eyes. "Well, how do we get it?"

Brice chewed his bottom lip in concentration. "Maybe magic?"

"Can't hurt to try it," Hollis stated. She and Reggie stepped back in case something backfired, but Sunny stayed right up beside Brice, expectation on her face.

Brice closed his eyes and concentrated. He focused on the magic within him. Different witches including Jessica Calloway, Ryne's mom, and Mathilde Augustine had been working with him little by little. He had been getting familiar with it in his free time and had been able to find it easier. He called on his magic and focused it on the wall. Brice focused on his intention to have the journal and placed his hand on the wall. Something depressurized underneath his hand and part of the wall separated and flung out toward him.

"You did it!" Sunny clapped, and the others rushed forward next to him. "Pull it out."

Brice's eyes were wide. He did it, he really did. He didn't see anything at first. "What if there's a trap or something, and it takes my hand off?"

Sunny laughed. Brice gave her a funny look, but he realized she still simply waited for him to do what he had come there to do. So he reached in and felt around. Sure enough, his hand touched something book-sized. He gently gripped it and pulled it out.

"The journal," he said with awe. The journal was a very old leather-bound book with a strip of red suede connected as a bookmark. On the cover of it was detailed metalwork that looked to be an opening for something to fit inside it. Brice gently ran his fingers over the cover.

He looked up and smiled at everyone there. "We did it."

He passed the journal to Sunny, but she bit her lip and shook her head. He handed it to his father, who examined the book for a moment and flipped open to the first few pages. "We need to be very gentle; this is extremely old."

"They're here," Aunt Letti shouted down the stairs.

"We're coming up," Reggie announced. "We should show it to everyone." He handed the book back to Brice, who cradled it protectively in his arms as they went back upstairs.

At the top, those who could get there on short notice had gathered in the lobby area. Brice took the time to take the journal around to his grandmother, his mother, his sister, his aunt, and his brother.

"What should we do with it?" Macy asked.

"Study it," Brice said. "Everything Marie and Judson knew has to be in here." He thumbed through to the end of the book. "Look, there's personal entries in here from Marie and from Judson too!"

"You study it, little brother, and let me know what's in there. With all my new classes at SMA, I'm not going to have the extra time to study that, too," Macy said, a bit disappointed.

"Is that all right with everyone, if I read it first?" Brice asked. His family all agreed, and he couldn't wait to get started. "One question I have that I don't think I need the journal for, because Mom has evaded it for many years . . ."

"What is that, son?" Lilith asked with hesitation.

"Why is my hair dark and I'm marked a hunter?"

"And Hollis's hair, too?" Macy threw in.

"From the little I've gleaned, when you kill a witch then proceed to have offspring marked as a hunter, their hair can turn dark as a part of the curse or evidence of your actions. It doesn't mean the same if you have human children, however," she said, giving a nod in Brock's direction.

"Interesting. I did not see that being the reason at all," Macy said, half disappointed.

"I have a question," Sunny spoke up. "Why did you give Brice and Macy the middle names of Marie and Dante?"

"Yeah, considering you already knew he was a bad guy when you had me?" Brice added. "I'm not sure why I never thought to ask about it. I just thought it was a family tradition type thing."

"Before both Brice and Macy were born, actually not too long after Brock was born, Mathilde Augustine came to us. She has witches with Seer powers in her ancestry, as you know, Gallad." Reggie looked at Gallad, who nodded. "Actually, Sunny, she might be someone you could talk with if you wanted. Anyway, she came to us and said she had a vision of two more children—a girl, then a boy. And she said their middle names were to be Marie and Dante."

Lilith smiled at her children and added the rest, "She also said they were to mark the beginning of a new era of witch hunters. They were to be key in having the truth of the Blackstone family rediscovered."

"And so they did," Sunny said with a big smile.

And so they did.

EPILOGUE

*B*rice spent all his free time over the past few weeks studying the Blackstone family journal, and he was surprised at some of the information he found. It took him some time, but with Sunny's help, he was able to learn how the dagger and the journal worked together to unlock more of the family secrets.

"What have you learned new, Brice?" Sunny asked one evening as she joined him by the fire in the great room of his family's home. He turned toward her, his face lit up with a smile, and said, "I found a section that told how a witch hunter extracts the magical essence from a dying witch and absorbs it for their own energy to preserve their life. But then Marie added her own experience, using the power of the dagger, along with Judson's magic, to not only pull the essence from someone who was very alive, but then send it back into their soul without hurting them. She only did it once, and it was to save the life of a young girl who was possessed by a demon who took over her body."

With her eyes wide, Sunny sat on the edge of the seat. "Did it work?"

"Yep, it was awesome!" Brice added, excited about what he had learned. Then his face fell. "It was much like what Dante had told me to do, but he didn't tell me it would kill the person whose magical energy I took."

"But you didn't. And that is what matters," Sunny encouraged, and with her, there was no argument. To change the subject, though, she added, "How are your magic lessons going?"

Brice's face lit up. "It's awesome! It is such an amazing feeling to have magic surge through my veins. But then, it's the weirdest feeling to have your own body wrestle with itself as the hunter tries to attack the magic. It's less and less, though, as I accept more of who I am and learn to control more each day. I think I might be able to get the hang of having the two coexist within me."

"You will," Sunny said with a wink, then got up and moved to the window. After a moment of quiet she asked, "Brice?"

"Hmm?" he looked up from the journal he studied once again.

"Did Dante tell you the vision I had of the two of you together?"

Brice stilled. "He did."

He hadn't brought up the vision with her yet, and truth be told, he hadn't wanted to, for fear of his destiny being entwined with Dante's.

"It wasn't about becoming his successor. It was about exactly what you have already done . . ."

"What's that, Sunny?" he asked quietly as he came up behind her.

"Replacing him in existence by having rediscovered your truth." She turned to him and smiled. Then, unexpectedly, she reached up on her tiptoes, swiped the dark hair from his eyes, and kissed him on the lips.

Brice laughed at the shock of electricity he felt shoot through him at their touch. "Rediscovered indeed."

And he kissed her again, this time with passion. When they came apart breathless and giggling, Brice held Sunny close to his chest with the lights of the town twinkling in the background.

"Are you ready?" he asked, with a suddenly serious expression on his face.

"Ready for what?" she asked, tilting her head, confused.

Brice gently pushed her away while still holding one of her hands so she extended out and away from him, then he tugged her quickly back into his embrace and smoothly transitioned into a gentle sway. She giggled as she clumsily stepped on his foot. But he didn't care. They were dancing.

"This is just how I saw it," she said and laid her head on his chest.

"Sunny, will you go to the Haunting on Main Street event with me for Halloween and then the Cold Moon Ball in December?"

"I will go with you always to every event you want to attend. We belong together, Brice Blackstone."

"Rediscovered indeed," Brice reiterated, then kissed the top of her head as they continued to sway into the night.

We hope you enjoyed this story in the Havenwood Falls High series of novellas featuring a variety of supernatural creatures. The series is a collaborative effort by multiple authors. Each author writes a stand-alone story, so you can read them in any order.

Other books in the Young Adult Havenwood Falls High series, in recommended order of reading (however, each author has written a stand-alone story, so they can be read in any order):

Shadows & Spells by Cameo Renae
Falling Deep by J.L. Weil
Saving Infiniti by Rose Garcia
Willful by Liz Ferry
Cast in Moonlight by Ali Winters
Promise the Moon by Kallie Ross
Blurred Lines by Daniele Lanzarotta
Ascending Darkness by J.L. Weil
Finding Infiniti by Rose Garcia
Unicorn's Lament by Megan Linski
Paper Bird by Amy Richie
Rediscovered by Morgan Wylie
Ashes of Fate by April Baker

More books releasing on a monthly basis. Stay up to date at www.HavenwoodFalls.com

Subscribe to our reader group and receive free stories and more!

ABOUT THE AUTHOR

Morgan Wylie is an award-winning and *USA Today* bestselling author with several genres published from YA fantasy to adult paranormal romance and other things in between. Morgan published her first novel, *Silent Orchids,* one year after moving across the country with her family on a journey of new discovery. After an amazing three years in Nashville, TN, and the release of two more books, Morgan and her family found their way back to the Northwest, where they now reside. Still working every day with great optimism, Morgan continues to embrace all things: "Mama," wife, teacher, and mediator to the many voices and muses constantly chattering in her head . . . where it gets pretty loud!

You can find her and news on her books at the following:

MorganWylie.net
MorganWylieBooks on Facebook
@MWylieBooks on Twitter/Instagram

ACKNOWLEDGMENTS

Writing in Havenwood Falls is such an incredible experience, and I'm honored to be a part of this community. Thank you, Kristie Cook, for allowing me such an opportunity.

Thank you to the following authors for the use of or mention of their characters: Kristie Cook for the use of Saundra Beaumont, Addie Beaumont, Aurelia and Michaela Petran; Kallie Ross for the use of Sheriff Ric Kasun; Liz Ferry for the mention of Celeste Long, Emma Cardin, and Jonathan Burns; R.K. Ryals for the mention of Cade Peters; E.J. Fechenda for the mention of Dalton and Dr. Underwood; Victoria Escobar for the mention of Remy MacKinnon; Amy Richie for the mention of Ava Tate; Amy Hale for the mention of Zoey Mills and Jordan Woods; Katie M. John for the mention of Ellie Lewis; and Cameo Renae for the mention of Weston and Drake Blaekthorn.

Thank you to Kristie Cook and Liz Ferry for your editing and proofreading expertise!

Thank you, David Uhlenkott, for your special assistance and expertise in the world of skateboarding and helping with terms and techniques!

Thank you to my wonderful, patient, and supportive family as I wrote this. I love you!

And last but not least thank you to YOU, the amazing reader that you are!! Thank you.

AN EXCERPT

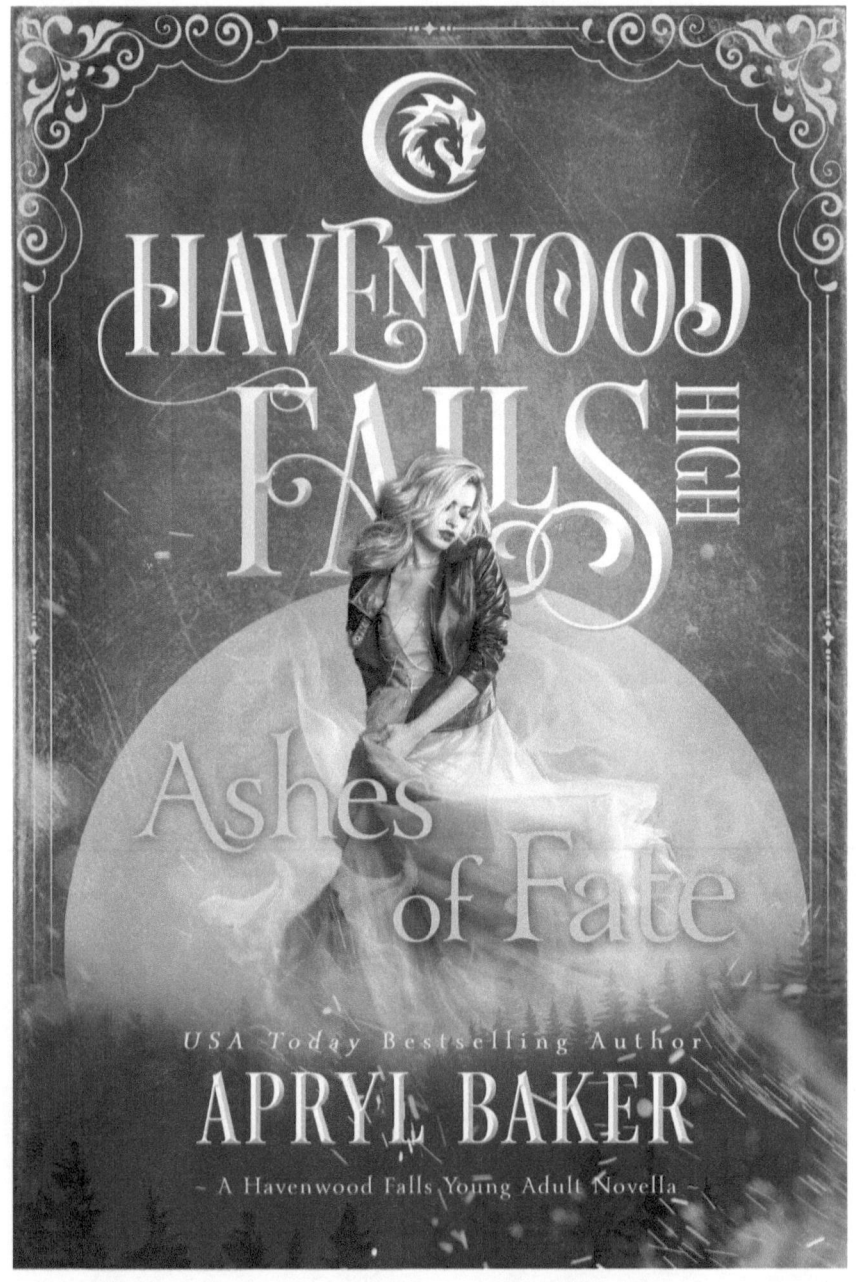

HAVENWOOD FALLS HIGH

Ashes of Fate

USA Today Bestselling Author

APRYL BAKER

~ A Havenwood Falls Young Adult Novella ~

AN EXCERPT

Ashes of Fate (**A Havenwood Falls High Novella) by April Baker**

From *USA Today* bestselling author Apryl Baker . . . A single random act. One swerve of a car. In a blink, it's all gone.

Cora Hartwood lost everything in a single heartbeat, and she's left with crushing guilt and dark thoughts that drive her to consider even darker ideas. She and her grandmother came to Havenwood Falls for a new start, to get away from the memories of the tragedy that took her family.

Or so she thought.

Her grandmother reveals that what happened to her family wasn't an accident. They were murdered, and the two of them fled to Havenwood Falls and the safety it offered. The secrets of her family's past are revealed, leaving Cora to question everything.

Now she's not only dealing with guilt, but she worries about becoming a victim to the same person who took her family from her. She's scared and falling apart.

Until she meets Reed Spencer.

He seems to understand the dark place she's in and brings a little light into her life. He's the one person she can turn to, and he's quickly becoming not only her friend, but something more.

But she's not as safe as she thinks, and it will take the magic of Havenwood Falls to save her.

ASHES OF FATE

BY APRYL BAKER

CHARLESTON, SC

"Cora!"

Cora Hartwood ignored her best friend's shout, instead focusing on the super cute Dracula sitting beside her. Seth Michaels had been flirting with her for three days and she'd finally worked up the courage to pull him into a semi-quiet corner of the biggest party of the year. Bonfires raged along the beach outside, but she'd never liked fire and chose to stay indoors.

Most everyone was out there, and she and Seth could cuddle and maybe make out a little. At least that was the plan, if Emily would shut up.

"You look hot as a zombie nurse," Seth whispered in Cora's ear, his teeth tugging at her earlobe. She shivered in response, loving the way he made her feel. Cora had made out with a couple guys before, but none of them gave her butterflies in her stomach like Seth did.

"You don't look so bad yourself, Count Dracula." Cora giggled and leaned in closer, snuggling up to Seth.

"Cora Jean Hartwood!"

The sheer desperation in Emily's voice startled her into looking away from Seth, her gaze finding Emily in a few seconds. She looked scared.

Cora pushed up from Seth, who called after her, and went running.

"What is it?" She grasped Emily's arm and pulled her friend around to face her. "Are you okay? Did somebody try something? Just tell me who and I'll . . ."

"No, not me!" Emily's dark brown eyes were wide with so many different emotions, Cora couldn't keep up. "The sheriff's here looking for you."

"Me?" Shock rippled through her. She'd been with some friends earlier but had left before they'd started to egg cars and houses. Surely someone hadn't called and reported her for hanging with them, making the sheriff think she was a part of that nonsense.

"Something happened, Cora, something bad. You need to come with me."

She refused to budge, a knot of fear beginning to twist in her stomach. "Tell me what's wrong."

"I . . . I don't know. Sheriff McCarty wouldn't say. He just said to find you and bring you out front."

"Cora?" Seth came to a stop beside her. "What's going on?"

"I don't know, but I have to go." She didn't even look at him, but followed Emily out of the beach house, her mind sorting through a million different what-ifs. The waves were crashing onto the sand, coming close to the bonfires, which blazed high. The fire held her attention for a brief moment. She hated fire, and right now, it seemed to mock her, to tease her that it was about to rob her of everything precious.

Shivering, she turned away and followed Emily down to where the sheriff's SUV was parked at the very edge of the property. He looked grim.

"Sheriff, this is Cora." Emily grabbed Cora's hand and held tight.

"Miss Hartwood, there's been an accident."

"Accident?" A new kind of fear curled in her stomach, and she got very, very cautious. "What kind of accident?"

"Your parents and brother were involved in a motor vehicle accident this evening. They've all been rushed to the hospital in critical condition."

Motor vehicle accident.

Her mind went blank, and she felt numb. The chill in the air disappeared as well as all the sounds around her. Emily's and the sheriff's faces faded away as those three little words swirled round and round in her head.

"Cora!"

Hands grabbed her as her body sagged. Her family was in an accident while she'd been making out at a party. She was supposed to have gone with them to the pumpkin patch and then to the haunted house in town. But she'd decided to go hang out with her friends instead.

She was supposed to have been in that car.

"Miss Hartwood?"

She blinked, her mind refocusing on the sheriff. "They're not dead?"

"I won't lie. It doesn't look good. We need to get you to the ER if you want to see them."

Cora nodded and took out her phone, texting her grandma. She lived in Florida, but she would find a way to get here. Cora only saw her grandma at Christmas, and they Skyped on birthdays, but despite not being as close as they could be, Hattie should know.

And Cora needed her.

Emily climbed into the back of the SUV with her, but Cora was barely aware of her. She kept thinking about her family. Her little brother had begged her to come with them, but she'd wanted to go to the party where all her friends were. She wanted to hang out with Seth instead of Billy. If she'd just been in the backseat of her parents' car, maybe she could have shielded Billy. Maybe he wouldn't have gotten hurt.

Emily snapped her fingers in front of Cora's face, bringing her out of her haze. "Your phone's ringing."

Cora stared at it. Her grandmother's face was on the screen. Even

117

though she'd texted her a few minutes ago, she couldn't bring herself to answer it. That would mean admitting out loud how bad the situation was.

Emily took the phone from her and answered it, explaining everything to her grandmother. Cora heard her, but it was like she was hearing her from the end of a long tunnel.

Shock. This had to be shock. Her body was in shock.

But she couldn't do anything to help herself.

"Cora, your grandmother said to tell you she'll be on the first flight she can get."

Cora nodded, her fingers twisting each other. Emily pulled her hands apart. "You're going to hurt yourself."

They rode in silence for the rest of the way, and when the sheriff pulled up in front of the ER, Cora's body refused to move. Emily sat with her and eventually coaxed her out, but a fear unlike anything she'd ever known crept up and took a hold of her.

Walking through the ER doors, she all but stopped breathing, holding onto Emily's hand so tightly, the circulation might have been cut off. The girls followed the sheriff to the information desk. The nurse looked over at her, her expression sympathetic and full of pity.

Cora's heart sank.

There would be no reason she'd give her that look unless it was bad. How bad remained to be seen.

They were escorted into the ER itself and into a small waiting area. A few other people were there, but they were told a doctor would be out to see them shortly.

"Wha . . . what happened? Can you tell me?"

"It looks like a hit and run," the sheriff said. "There was a witness to the accident who called 9-1-1. The car in front of the witness was going really fast and swerved into your parents' lane. They hit your family head on. The witness said it looked like your father lost control and spun out, slamming into the guard rail, and flipped, forcing the car over the rail and into the ravine. We have an APB out with the car's description and the partial plate number the witness was able to provide."

Cora nodded. A random act. One swerve and it cost her family so much.

A man wearing scrubs came out a few minutes later. He walked straight to her, his expression kind. "Miss Hartwood?"

"Yes." Cora stood, still clutching Emily's hand like a lifeline.

"I'm Dr. Hall. We've got your parents stable, but they both need surgery. I need you to sign a consent since you're the next of kin."

"My gran is on her way. She's getting the first flight out."

"We don't have time to wait. If we don't operate now, they'll die."

"They'll live if you do?" Cora whispers.

"I can't promise you that. Their injuries are severe, but surgery is their best option."

"And my brother?"

"I'm sorry. He died before he got to the hospital."

"No." Cora didn't recognize the sound that escaped her. It was a half cry, half moan. Her knees weakened, and she sank back down.

"I'm very sorry," the doctor said. "I hate to ask this of you, but we need to go now if we're going to save them."

Why would they ask her to do this? It wasn't fair. She was only seventeen. She shouldn't have to make this decision.

"Miss Hartwood?" the doctor prompted when she didn't answer.

"Okay. Please, just don't let them die. Please."

Papers were handed to her, and she signed them blindly.

"Can I see them before you go into surgery?"

"I'm afraid not. We need to get them into surgery now."

Again, she nodded and watched the doctor walk away.

Emily squeezed her hand. "It's going to be okay, Cora."

"It's not. Billy died. My brother died." Tears started leaking, and once the waterworks began, they wouldn't stop.

Emily hugged her close, whispering things Cora didn't hear.

All she could think about was her brother and her parents as they sat and waited for the doctor to come back.

Purchase *Ashes of Fate* where books are sold.

www.ingramcontent.com/pod-product-compliance
Lightning Source LLC
Chambersburg PA
CBHW020408130626
46549CB00006B/2477